DUFFEL BAGS AND DROWNINGS

By

Dorothy Howell

ISBN: 978-0-9856930-2-2

Published in the United States of America

DUFFEL BAGS AND DROWNINGS

With love to Stacy, Judy, Seth, and Brian

I couldn't have written this novella without the support of a lot of people. Some of them are: Stacy Howell, Judith Branstetter, David Howell, Martha Cooper, Evie Cook, Webcrafters Design, and William F. Wu, Ph.D.

Special thanks to the readers and friends who contributed the lawyer jokes: Carol Beyner, Gina Cresse, Joyce Meyer, Marilynn Stella, and all the others who wished to remain anonymous.

.

Mysteries by Dorothy Howell

The Haley Randolph Mystery Series
Handbags and Homicide
Purses and Poison
Shoulder Bags and Shootings
Clutches and Curses
Slay Bells and Satchels
Tote Bags and Toe Tags
Evening Bags and Executions
Duffel Bags and Drownings
Beach Bags and Burglaries
Fanny Packs and Foul Play

The Dana Mackenzie Mystery Series
Fatal Debt
Fatal Luck

DUFFEL BAGS AND DROWNINGS

By

Dorothy Howell

Dorothy Howell

Chapter 1

"Something major is going down," Kyla murmured. "Have you heard anything?"

I hadn't but, of course, I wanted to.

"What's up?" I asked, filling my cup from the giant coffee maker on the counter.

We were squeezed into the breakroom of L.A. Affairs, the event planning company where we both worked as assistant planners, along with a dozen or so other employees all intent on delaying the start of our work day by spending an inordinate amount of time chatting about what we'd done the night before, what we planned to do today, and how we were going to get out of most of it—or maybe that was just me.

Kayla glanced around, then whispered, "Priscilla stopped Edie in the hallway."

Kayla--tall, dark haired, and about my age—had worked here longer that I had, so no way would I completely dismiss her warning. Still, the office manager stopping the head of H.R. in the hallway first thing in the morning, while troubling, was no reason to panic—especially before I'd had my first cup of breakroom-stalling-to-get-to-work coffee.

"They were whispering," Kayla said.

Okay, whispering in the hallway definitely amped things up. But, again, no need to panic. I, Haley Randolph, with my long pageant legs stretching me to an

3

enviable five-foot-nine, my doesn't-it-make-me-look-smart dark hair, and my I'm-staring-down-25-years-old-and-not-panicking outlook on life, had been through this sort of thing before and knew it could mean absolutely nothing.

In the past few years I'd worked more than my share of jobs: life guard, receptionist, file clerk, and two weeks at a pet store. Add to that a bang-up job in the accounting department of the prestigious we-could-take-over-the-world Pike Warner law firm that could have worked out well for me if it hadn't been for that whole administrative-leave-investigation-pending thing—long story. I'd landed at yet another fabulous company—another long story—where things hadn't worked out exactly as I'd hoped—none of which was my fault, of course.

The only job I'd managed to hold onto was a crappy part-time sales clerk position at the equally crappy Holt's Department Store which I intended to ditch—complete with the take-this-job-and-shove-it speech I'd rehearsed since my second day of employment there and the series of Olympic caliber cartwheels and backflips I intended to execute on the way out of their front door—as soon as my probation was up at L.A. Affairs.

The office was located in a high rise at Sepulveda and Ventura Boulevards in the upscale area of Sherman Oaks, part of Los Angeles, amid other office buildings, banks, apartment complexes, and the terrific shops and restaurants just across the street at the Sherman Oaks Galleria. L.A. Affairs prided itself for its reputation as event planners to the stars, catering to upscale clients, the rich and famous, the power brokers and insiders of Los Angeles and Hollywood—plus anyone else who could afford our astronomical fees.

"It could be nothing," I said, emptying a packet of sugar into my coffee.

"Or it could be *something*," Kayla said, as she poured herself a cup. She gave me a quick nod over her shoulder. "Listen."

I noticed then that the early morning chatter in the breakroom was more subdued than usual. Not a good sign.

I dumped two more sugars into my cup.

Eve, another assistant planner, wormed her way between Kayla and me. Eve was a petite redhead who was a few years older than me. She was a huge gossip so, of course, I'd become her BFF right away.

"Oh my God, something's up," Eve said, as she fumbled to fill her coffee cup. "Something big."

Kayla and I immediately leaned closer.

"What have you heard?" Kayla whispered.

"Nothing," Eve told us. "It's what I *saw*."

Kayla and I exchanged a this-is-definitely-something-major eyebrow bob.

"Priscilla and Edie were whispering in the hallway," Eve said. She paused, indicating the worst part of her story was about to be revealed, and said, "Then they went into Edie's office."

Oh my God. Kayla had been right. Something major was definitely going down. I grabbed two more sugar packets and dumped them into my coffee.

"And," Eve announced, holding Kayla and me both in but-wait-there's-more suspense, "they closed the door."

Oh, yeah. This was bad, all right.

"Do you think they're going to lay someone off?" Kayla asked.

"Or fire someone," Eve said. "Maybe more than one person."

"Several people?" Kayla asked, shaking her head. "Who?"

Kayla and Eve both turned to me, and I got an all-too-familiar sick feeling in my belly. I'd been one of the last people hired at L.A. Affairs. Did that mean I'd be one of the first to go?

"Maybe they'll fire Vanessa," I said, and tried for a this-could-work-out-great smile.

Vanessa Lord was the senior planner I was assigned to—though we almost never spoke. She hated me, and I hated her back, of course. Vanessa brought the biggest clients to the firm, which made her the biggest bitch in the firm, unfortunately.

"They'll never let Vanessa go," Kayla said. She managed a small smile. "But we can always hope."

"Keep your eyes open and your heads down today," Eve advised and left.

"Let me know if you hear anything," Kayla said, as she grabbed her coffee and headed out of the breakroom.

I topped off my cup with a generous amount of French vanilla creamer befitting the stress of the morning, and followed her out. In the hallway, I saw that the door to Edie's office was still closed. Not a good sign. I paused as I passed by—which was kind of bad of me, I know—and leaned closer. I heard murmurs but nothing specific—like my name being bandied about—so I went to my office.

I loved my office, my private sanctuary. It had a neutral desk, chair, bookcase, and credenza, and was accented with vibrant shades of blues and yellows. My favorite part was the large window that gave me a fabulous view of the Galleria across the street, and the surrounding area.

I had plenty of work to do, all sorts of events that I was in various stages of planning, but no way could I face them right now, not with this whole somebody-could-get-the-axe-today-and-it-could-be-me thing hanging over my head.

I walked to the window and looked down at the traffic creeping along the crowded streets, and the people rushing to get wherever they were going, and sipped my coffee. I had to admit to myself that this was an occasion when still having an official boyfriend to talk to would be good.

Ty Cameron was my last official boyfriend. He was absolutely gorgeous, super smart, organized, competent and professional, the fifth generation of his family to run the chain of Holt's Department Stores. If we were still together I could call him, talk this over, and he'd make me feel better—if he wasn't in a meeting, or on an international conference call, and had time to talk, of course.

We'd broken up for obvious reasons.

I sipped my coffee and thought about calling my best friend Marcie Hanover. She worked at a bank in downtown Los Angeles and was always available to discuss a problem, a fabulous new handbag I'd seen, or just about anything, as a BFF would.

But this didn't seem like a good time to call her.

It seemed like a good time to leave.

No way did I want to be around when Edie's office door opened, she and Priscilla walked out with personnel folders in their hands—possibly one with my name on it— and started calling people in. So naturally, fleeing my private sanctuary was the only thing to do.

I got my handbag—a terrific Chanel bag that

perfectly accessorized my awesome navy blue business suit—grabbed an event portfolio, and left.

***

I got my Honda from the parking garage and headed west on Ventura Boulevard toward Encino. Traffic wasn't bad, considering, so it didn't take long before I reached the shopping center where Cady Faye Catering, my excuse to get out of the office, was located.

As I made the left turn into their parking lot, a black Land Rover pulled out of the driveway and turned right. I caught a glimpse of the driver. Oh my God, it was Jack Bishop. I nearly ran up on the curb.

Jack Bishop was a private detective, the hottest hottie in P.I. hot-land. Tall, dark haired, rugged build, and really good looking. I'd helped him out on some of his cases and he'd returned the favor a few times—strictly professional, of course.

For a couple of seconds I considered doing a whip-around and following Jack—just to be sociable, of course—but it was a total high school move and I couldn't quite bring myself to do it. I did wonder, though, why Jack had been at this shopping center.

Was he on a case? A stakeout? Maybe involved in some high-stakes, international, super-secret job?

His life was so much cooler than mine.

I glanced at the businesses that occupied the complex with Cady Faye Catering—a dry cleaners, a real estate office, a dentist, a scrapbooking store, a gift shop, a nail place, and a restaurant specializing in vegetarian tacos. I preferred to think that a totally hot private detective wouldn't shop at any of those places, but I guess even Jack

Bishop needed to get his teeth cleaned or his shirts pressed.

I cruised past the stores and the large display window that had "Cady Faye Catering" printed on it in large white letters. I'd been inside their shop on my first visit here a few weeks ago and knew there were comfortable seating areas, books with photos taken at previous Cady Faye catered events, all set in tasteful décor befitting their upscale clientele.

Cady Faye Catering had built a great reputation over the past few years and had asked to be added to the L.A. Affairs' list of approved vendors. None of the other planners had wanted to take a chance on them. L.A. Affairs lived or died by its reputation so none of the planners wanted to make a mistake—and possibly lose their job—by giving something as important as the selection of the caterer to a company no one had worked with before.

I'd learned about Cady Faye—owned and operated by two sisters, Cady Wills and Faye Delaney—a few months ago when I'd stopped by my parents' house as the caterers were setting up for one of Mom's dinner parties. My mom was a former pageant queen—really—who thought she was still a pageant queen, so no way would she cook for her own party. She'd never complained about Cady Faye's food or service—and believe me, if Mom hadn't liked anything about them she'd have said so multiple times—which assured me they'd done a great job.

I'd gone to Priscilla, the office manager at L.A. Affairs, and told her I'd like to give Cady Faye a try. Priscilla had given me raised eyebrows and a slow headshake, but I'd persisted. The more Priscilla had resisted, the more I'd wanted to use them—which I prefer to think of as my generous spirit, not the mile-wide stubborn streak some people have mentioned, as if it were a personality flaw. Priscilla had finally given in and agreed to let me use them, but I'd gotten a this-better-work-out grimace from her.

I could have tried out Cady Faye Catering on a small, simple event, but I'd gone with something bigger—a St. Patrick's Day party being given by Xander and Nadine Brannock, a young, up and coming Hollywood couple. I'd figured that at a rip-roaring St. Pat's bash I could see how Cady Faye operated—plus hardly any of the guests would be sober enough the next day to remember the food at all.

I circled to the back of the shopping center and parked at the rear entrance alongside two of Cady Faye's delivery vans. Nearby were a truck unloading bread and a van from Maisie's Costume Shop, as well as a couple dozen other vehicles. Another catering delivery van was backed up to the open double doors. Cady Faye was expanding so construction work was underway on both sides of their shop. I grabbed my portfolio and squeezed past the delivery van into their small receiving area.

Inside, a line of workers in white smocks and hairnets carried boxes and trays to the van, preparing to head out for a luncheon somewhere, apparently. A dozen or so guys and girls—servers, I figured, since they looked like college students—milled around, some wearing a Cady Faye Catering uniform, others in street clothes. Construction workers hauled around equipment. The place smelled like sawdust and fresh baked bread.

I spotted Faye Delaney right away. She was an average looking late-thirties gal with sensible hair and comfortable shoes. She was talking to a leprechaun—or, at least, a young woman in a leprechaun costume.

The costume was beyond cool—green vest, bow tie,

and jacket over a white shirt, green below-the-knee pants, green and white striped knee socks, and black buckle shoes. The girl looked great in it. She was a couple of years younger than me, tall with brown hair. She'd probably look great in anything

Neither she nor Faye looked happy.

As I walked closer I heard Faye say, "I don't know why she can't get here on time. Especially today. She knows full well that—"

"Oh, hi," the leprechaun said to me, cutting Faye off.

Faye spotted me and instantly morphed into everything's-great mode.

"Haley, so good to see you," she said, smiling broadly. She gestured to the leprechaun beside her. "This is Jeri Sutton, one of my hardest working employees. She's trying on the costume for the Brannock party for me. What do you think?"

"Looks great," I said.

"Maisie's Costume Shop is here fitting the servers," Faye said, and managed a brave smile. "On top of everything else that's going on."

I glanced around at the hustle and bustle that bordered on chaos.

"But it's nothing we can't handle," Faye said.

"I'll go look for Cady," Jeri said. "Somebody said they thought they saw her here a few minutes ago."

"Thank you, Jeri," Faye said, and exhaled heavily. "But don't be gone too long. I need you to model that costume with a skirt."

Jeri moved away and Faye said to me, "She's one of my trusted agents. I don't know what I'd do without her. She's in culinary school, you know."

I didn't, but Faye kept talking before I could say

anything.

"Let me show you our newest toy." She talked as we walked, telling me about upcoming events.

The place was a bit of a maze, since they'd taken over the stores on each side of their original shop. Construction workers, the catering staff and servers were coming and going as we passed storage rooms, the huge kitchen, a cool room, and a utility room and janitor's closet.

Faye stopped at the entrance to one of the rooms and gestured grandly.

"The ice room," she announced. "We're the first catering company in the area to have one."

I walked inside. Bare walls, a concrete floor, harsh overhead lighting, several chest freezers, and some sort of hoist. There was a big open water tank sitting atop a metal frame about eight feet off the floor with steps leading up to it and hoses sprouting from it.

I guess Faye picked up on my where's-the-ice expression because she said, "It's for making ice sculptures."

"I thought they were cut out of big blocks of ice with a chain saw," I said.

"They can be, but look." Faye opened a big metal door across the room. Inside was a huge walk-in freezer and shelves lined with dozens of ice sculptures ranging in size from a few inches to several feet—green shamrocks, stars, leprechauns, rainbows, and just about everything else Irish you could think of.

"Cool," I said. "These will look great at the party."

"We can make them for any occasion," Faye said. "Let me tell you how it's done."

She closed the freezer door and launched into an explanation of how colored water was mixed in the big

12

tank, then pumped into rubber molds and lowered into chest freezers by a hoist, and then everything turned into blah-blah-blah and I drifted off.

That happens a lot.

Edie, Priscilla, and whatever the heck was going on at L.A. Affairs popped into my head. I wondered if I could find a way to stay out of the office for the rest of the day. Maybe tomorrow, too. I mean, jeez, if I wasn't there, they couldn't fire me, right?

Faye jarred me back to reality by walking away. I followed, pulled the door closed, and we headed toward what I thought was the front of building—my sense of direction isn't the greatest—where the display room and offices were located.

We stopped at the entrance to the employee lounge. Inside were tables and chairs, vending machines, a fridge and microwave. On one wall was a bulletin board pinned with announcements, and on another ran a row of lockers; duffel bags and backpacks were piled up under them.

Near the restrooms, two clothing racks held leprechaun costumes. Guy servers rotated in and out trying them on, while the girls sat idle at the tables. I'd worked with Maisie's Costume Shop on other events and knew they'd do a great job.

Maisie, a stout woman in her forties who owned the shop, checked the fit on each server as they came out of the restroom, and her assistant Wendy entered their sizes on her iPad.

"Hey, Haley," Wendy called.

Like most of the wardrobe people I'd met, Wendy had a fashion-forward sense of style that bordered on outrageous. Today she had on boots, tights, shorts, a tank, and vest in progressive shades of purple. But since she probably didn't weigh a hundred pounds on a rainy day, she really pulled it off.

Faye's cell phone rang. She stepped away and answered it.

"Awesome costumes," I said.

Wendy gestured toward the clothing racks. "We brought skirts for the girls. Jeri is going to try on one so we can see how it looks. What do you think?"

"I think it will be great," I said, "as long as the servers don't look better than the guests."

Wendy laughed, then stopped as Fay's voice rose.

"She didn't get back to you?" she said into her phone. "She assured me she would. I'm so sorry. I'll get on it right away. Yes, of course. You have my word."

Faye snapped her phone closed and exclaimed, "Has anyone seen Cady?"

"Wasn't she here just a minute ago?" someone asked.

"I thought I saw her car out front when I came in," one of the girls said.

"Well, is she here, or not?" Faye asked, looking more annoyed by the second. "And where is Jeri? She's supposed to try on the skirt with her costume. Why aren't people here, where they're supposed to be? Things have to get done."

"I'll look for them," one of the girls said.

"Me, too," another one added.

"All of you," Faye said, "please, look for them. And tell them to report back to me immediately."

Faye blew out a big breath as the girls hurried out of the room, then caught sight of me standing nearby.

"Oh, Haley," she said. "Please don't think this sort of thing happens often. Really, we're all dedicated to the success of this business. I'm sure Cady is here somewhere and she's anxious to go over the menu with you."

"No problem," I said.

I thought there definitely was a problem but this didn't seem like the time to say so.

"I'll look for them, too," I said.

Honestly, I didn't know how I'd have any better luck finding Cady and Jeri than anyone else, but it seemed like a great excuse to get away and call Kayla at the office to see if there'd been any new developments.

I walked along the hallways amid the hustle and bustle of the people who were doing actual work, and called Kayla's cell phone. Her voicemail picked up so I left a message. I tried the office line. Her voicemail picked up there, too.

Yikes! Did that mean Kayla was in with Edie and Priscilla getting fired? Of course, if that happened, it might be safe for me to go back to the office.

I mean that in the nicest way, of course.

I tucked my cell phone into my handbag and strolled along, trying to look as if I intended to actually accomplish something. It did seem weird that both Cady and Jeri were nowhere to be found. Maybe they'd both slipped out to a nearby Starbuck—I'd done that myself a time or two during the workday.

I opened doors along the hallway and peered inside. One was a storage closet containing plates, glasses, bowls and cups. Nobody there. The next door was linen storage; plenty of tablecloths and napkins but no people. The one after that was the ice room. I pulled the door open and looked inside. No one there either, except—

Something was strange about the room. I heard water dripping.

I got a weird feeling

Water pooled on the floor under the big tank. I hadn't noticed that when I was in here earlier.

My weird feeling got weirder.

I looked up and saw a black shoe sticking out of the water tank. Yikes!

I raced up the stairs. Facedown in the water was a leprechaun. Dead.

Chapter 2

I'd been involved with a few murder investigations in the past—long story—and homicide detectives had always wanted to talk with me simply because I'd had the misfortune of being in the wrong place at the wrong time. Today was no exception. After all, I'd discovered the body. And it didn't help that the sleeves of my fabulous navy blue suit jacket—now hanging in the women's restroom--were dripping with the same water in which the victim had died.

After spotting Jeri in her leprechaun costume floating in the water tank, I'd pulled her out. I'd hoped that maybe, somehow, she was still alive. But then I'd seen the scratches on her face and the big dent in her skull.

So here I was seated across the table from Detective Elliston, one of LAPD's finest, in a small conference room at Cady Faye Catering. Elliston had seen 50, easily, but hadn't seen the inside of a gym lately. He seemed anxious for his partner to arrive so he could get this interview over with—and, I suspected, have lunch.

"So, let's go over this one more time, Miss Randolph," Detective Elliston murmured, consulting the little notebook in his hand. "You arrived here at—"

A blood curdling scream sounded from outside the conference room. Oh my God, had somebody else been found dead?

Detective Elliston turned his head in that direction. I

bolted out of my chair and flew through the door into the shop's display room.

Standing just inside the shop entrance, surrounded by several people, was Cady Wills, sister of Faye Delaney, the "Cady" in "Cady Faye Catering." Cady was the same size and shape as her sister, but with blonde hair rather than brown, and she was in the throes of an all-out hysterical rant.

"She's dead? *Dead?* Jeri's *dead?*" Cady screamed. She flung out her arms, then plastered her hands on her head. "She can't be *dead!*"

Everyone around Cady tried to calm her, but she wasn't having it. Her screams grew louder. I was tempted to bitch-slap her—just to get her to calm down, of course—but her sister Faye showed up and led her away.

As her screams faded into the bowels of the building, I walked over to a young woman who'd stayed behind. I'd seen her here on my previous visits, but had never officially met her.

"Are you okay?" I asked.

I figured her for a couple of years older than me, maybe, short with dark hair. Pretty—except for the stunned expression on her colorless face.

She shook her head. "I didn't mean to upset Cady like that. She walked in so I told her. I mean, I had to tell her, didn't I? Somebody had to tell her."

"You work here, right?" I asked.

"Lourdes Vaughn," she said. "I'm Faye's assistant."

I guess I should have figured that, given that she had on nice pants, blouse, and blazer, and wasn't wearing a hairnet.

"I'm sure Cady will feel better after she goes home and gets some rest," I said.

I had no idea if that would help or not, but it seemed like the right thing to say.

"With all the work we have scheduled for today? No way will Faye let her leave," Lourdes said. "Besides, Cady wouldn't get any rest at home. Not with that husband of hers."

That didn't sound good.

Lourdes glanced toward the hallway that led to the rear of the shop. "I hope Faye won't be mad at me for telling her," she said.

"Did you know Jeri well?" I asked.

Annoyance flashed across Lourdes' face. "I'm afraid so," she told me. "Everybody knew Jeri well. She made sure of it."

Lourdes huffed irritably, then turned to me and gasped, as if really seeing me for the first time.

Oh, you're Haley. From L.A. Affairs. Sorry, I didn't recognize you right away."

She was in all-out back-pedal mode now, anxious to make a good impression on me, the person who'd given Cady Faye Catering their big break.

It was kind of cool.

"Look, this is all probably nothing," Lourdes said. "I don't see how Jeri could have been murdered, like the cops are saying. I mean, lots of people didn't really like her but that doesn't mean somebody—somebody *here*—actually killed her. Who would dislike her that much?"

Good question.

"Miss Randolph?" Detective Elliston called.

I turned and saw him standing outside the conference room next to—oh, wow, some really hot looking guy. He was in his early thirties, I figured, a little over six feet tall with a muscular build, blond hair and—oh wow again—

deep blue eyes.

"My partner, Detective Grayson," Elliston said.

"Dan Grayson," he said, and offered his hand.

I took it. Heat raced up my arm.

"She found the victim," Elliston said. "Haley Randolph."

Dan nodded. "We'll need a few more minutes of your—Randolph? Haley Randolph?"

The heat that had consumed me turned to ice.

"*The* Haley Randolph?" Dan asked, frowning.

Oh, crap.

Yeah, okay, I had a bit of a reputation with the LAPD. It was because of those other homicide detectives I'd met during past investigations—long story.

"Let's get this over with," I said, then put my nose in the air—one of the few traits I'd inherited from my pageant queen mom—and glided into the conference room.

I took a seat at the table. The detectives sat side by side across from me.

"I've heard about you down at headquarters," Dan said.

I don't think he meant that as a compliment.

"Then you've probably also heard that I'm better at solving murders than some of the detectives," I told him, and refrained, somehow, from doing a fist-pump.

A tiny grin pulled at his lips—which I only noticed because he was sitting directly across from me, I swear.

"Tell us what happened," Dan said, shifting into serious-cop mode.

"Faye needed to find Cady and Jeri, so I and some other people went looking for them," I said, trying to make it sound routine.

"But you're the only one who looked in the ice room," Dan pointed out. "Why is that?"

I'd learned a long time ago that the less said to a homicide detective, the better—for me, anyway. So no way was I going to let this interview get bogged down with a lot of unnecessary details.

"You'd have to ask the others why they didn't look there," I said.

"Why did you come here today?" Dan asked.

This didn't seem like the best time to mention that perhaps my job at L.A. Affairs was hanging in the balance, and that hiring Cady Faye Catering for a huge event had put me out on a very shaky limb.

"A routine call," I said.

Dan glanced at the notebook Elliston had placed on the table. "You're coordinating a big party for some important Hollywood people, aren't you? Were you worried about the success of your event?"

Of course I was.

"Of course not," I said.

No way was I admitting anything to two homicide detectives looking for a suspect.

"There's a lot of pressure on you to make these parties come off flawlessly," Dan said, and made it sound like I was on the bomb squad.

"Your job was at stake, wasn't it?" Dan went on. "You and the victim got into a confrontation."

"No," I told him. Okay, now I was starting to get rattled.

"Things got out of control," Dan said. "You hit her."

"I did not," I said. Yeah, I was really rattled now.

"She fell into the water tank and you left her there to die," Dan said.

"Of course not!"

Jeez, I'm usually better at this sort of thing. Something about this guy had me all keyed up.

He leaned closer. "There was no trail of water leading from the ice room. And you're the only person in the entire building whose clothing is wet. How do you explain that, Miss Randolph? How?"

I drew in a breath and tried to calm myself. Honestly, I'm not very good at calming myself, so what could I do but shift the conversation in a different direction?

"There're all kinds of exits from this place," I told him. "There's construction going on so things are wide open. People are all over the place—the builders, catering staff, servers, the costume people, delivery guys—and none of them know who's supposed to be here and who's not. Anybody could have slipped in and out unnoticed. Have you looked at the surveillance tape?"

Both detectives just stared at me.

"And tell me this," I demanded. "How the heck could killing somebody at my caterer cause my event to go smoother?"

Neither of them said anything, which suited me fine.

I shot to my feet and said, "If you have any more questions, you can call my lawyer."

I stomped to the door, stone-faced, hoping nothing about my expression revealed that I didn't actually have an attorney.

Detective Grayson called my name. I turned around. He was on his feet, his chest puffed out, his nose slightly flared—which is a totally hot look on men—and said, "You're involved in a murder investigation, Miss Randolph. Don't leave town."

I gave him what I hoped was a defiant glare—which

I'm afraid was actually an I-think-you're-really-hot glare—and left the room.

I headed toward the rear of the building, more than a little rattled. I desperately needed my all-time favorite drink, a mocha frappuccino from Starbucks. But since this place was, after all, a catering business, I figured I could find a suitable chocolate substitute in their kitchen.

I mean, really, if you can't pilfer something sweet after finding a dead body, when can you?

I headed for the cool room where the desserts and salads were prepared, but got lost in the maze of hallways and ended up at the employee lounge. Vending machine candy would do nicely, I decided, and walked inside.

The place was oddly quiet, after the hustle and bustle of the earlier costume fittings. I figured the police had already gotten the info they needed from the servers. The duffel bags and backpacks were all gone, except for one, so I guessed most everyone had gone home or, hopefully, was headed to the catering event the staff had been loading the vans for when I drove up.

Wendy stood at the clothing racks, going through the costumes and consulting her iPad. I headed straight for the vending machines.

"This is crazy, isn't it?" Wendy said. "I mean, Jeri dying? Do you think maybe it was, you know, an accident? She wasn't really murdered?"

"All I know is what the cops are saying," I said, as I pulled a ten from my wallet and fed it into the vending machine. "Want something?"

Wendy walked over. "Sure. How about a—oh my God, I love your handbag!"

I held up my Chanel satchel—it was a fabulous bag, and believe me, I know a fabulous bag when I see one—

and we spent a minute or so admiring it, a welcome break from talking about Jeri's murder.

"Have you seen the new Flirtatious?" Wendy asked.

My senses jumped to high alert. A new handbag was out? And I hadn't seen it?

"*Elle* is featuring it this month," Wendy said. "I got my issue this morning."

That explained why I hadn't heard about it. My issue was probably in my mailbox waiting for me.

I whipped out my cell phone and Googled it. A few seconds later the Flirtatious appeared on my phone. Wendy crowded close and we stood in reverent silence admiring it, a gorgeous yellow leather satchel perfect for spring and summer.

"I'm getting it," I said, the image burning into my brain.

"Really?" Wendy asked, dragging her gaze from my phone to my face. "It costs a fortune."

"Handbags are my vice," I admitted. "I don't smoke or do drugs. I buy handbags."

"Cigarettes and drugs would probably be cheaper," Wendy said.

I couldn't disagree.

I forwarded the Flirtatious link to Marcie, as a best friend would, and started pushing buttons on the vending machine. I gathered the candy from the delivery tray, passed some to Wendy, and we sat down at a table.

"Maisie's going to be really ticked off," she said, ripping open a Snickers bar and nodding toward the racks of costumes. "One of the leprechaun outfits was stolen."

I tore into a bag of M&Ms and poured most of it in my mouth.

"I wonder if any of the police are still here?" Wendy

said, glancing toward the door. "Maybe I should tell them."

"There's no such thing as costume police," I said.

Wendy bit into the candy bar. "Even if the guy brought it back later, it's still wrong to just take it."

I gulped down the M&Ms.

"Wait," I said, as the chocolate super-charged my brain. "A costume is missing? Other than Jeri's?"

Wendy nodded. "It's crappy, you know, not turning it in, keeping it for himself to wear on St. Patrick's Day."

"It was a guy?" I asked. "How do you know?"

Wendy touched the screen of her iPad. "It was a size extra-large. Only two of the guys needed that size."

My brain cells starting popping. I shoved the rest of the M&Ms in my mouth. One of the servers—a big guy— had been so anxious to leave the place he'd run out in a costume, looking like a giant leprechaun?

"Maybe he'll bring it back," Wendy said. "Maybe he had a family emergency, or something, and had to leave right away."

Ideas pinged around in my brain as I finished off the M&Ms—none of them involving a family emergency— and I pointed to the lone, green duffel bag sitting under the lockers I'd spotted when I walked in.

"If he left in such a hurry he didn't have time to change out of his costume," I said, "maybe he left that duffel bag behind."

"Yeah," Wendy agreed. "His name is probably in it and I can contact him to get the costume back before Maisie finds out."

My heart rate amped up as I grabbed the duffel bag and placed it on the table. Oh my God, could this really belong to the guy who murdered Jeri? I couldn't believe the cops had overlooked it.

I flashed on calling Detectives Grayson and Elliston, insisting they come here in person, then presenting them with the major break in the case that I'd discovered.

Cool.

There was no name tag on the strap of the duffel bag, so I unzipped it, visions of I'm-a-better-detective-than-you dancing in my head. I looked inside and my spirits fell.

"Damn," I muttered, as I pulled out a black lacy teddy and a handful of sexy lingerie.

Wendy sighed. "Well, I guess somebody is going to have a great getaway."

I shoved the clothing into the duffel bag and tossed it onto the floor where I'd found it.

Yeah, okay, my brilliant idea to solve the murder hadn't panned out, but oh well. It was really up to the detectives anyway.

Still, I couldn't imagine an emergency big enough to cause an extra-large guy to run around in a leprechaun costume—unless he'd just murdered someone.

Chapter 3

I'd had enough of Cady Faye Catering for one day, but I couldn't leave without talking to Faye. The Brannocks' party was coming up in a few days. I had to make sure the staff was still up to handling the event.

I found Faye in her office, a windowless, cramped space furnished with thrift store cast-offs, where she was frowning at a spreadsheet on her computer.

I rapped on the doorframe. Faye looked up.

"Haley, please come in and sit down," she said, with the same forced smile I'd seen on her face before. It was starting to freak me out.

Faye hopped up and moved a stack of file folders off a plastic chair in front of her desk. Even though there was little room to work, everything seemed neat and well organized. Faye had personalized the space by adding what I figured were family photos, shots of her, a man, and two tweens who must have been her husband and daughters. They were at the beach, gathered around a Christmas tree, and squeezed together at a picnic table.

"I'll be so glad when all this construction is finished," Faye said. "We so desperately need the space. I've tripled our business in the past year, you know."

"How is Cady?" I asked, sitting down.

Fay rounded her desk and dropped into her chair. "Resting, resting, resting. Cady always needs rest."

"She was really upset about Jeri," I said. "Were they

close?"

"Cady was just being Cady," Faye said, and waved her hands as if her sister's hysterical breakdown were nothing. "Completely over the top in her reaction to the news. She missed the entire episode, as usual, off somewhere doing something else, then falls to pieces in front of everyone. Typical."

"So she wasn't here earlier?" I asked. "Someone said they'd seen her car in the parking lot."

"She drives a white Mercedes. There must be hundreds of them on the streets. Obviously, someone else's car was mistaken for hers." Faye paused, squeezed her eyes shut for a few seconds, then looked at me again. "I can't believe this has happened—to Jeri, of all people."

I remembered that Faye had referred to Jeri as a trusted agent, although Lourdes didn't seem to think very highly of her.

"Was she a big part of your business?" I asked.

"Jeri was a hard worker, very anxious to learn all aspects of the business," Faye said. "And believe me, I can use all the help I can get."

"Any idea who might have killed her?" I asked.

Faye sat back in her chair and shook her head. "None whatsoever. I can't imagine anyone here would do such a thing. I know my employees, and none of them are capable of something like this."

I figured that Faye, like most business owners and supervisors, didn't know her employees nearly as well as she thought. In fact, people in Faye's position were usually the last to know if there was a problem among the employees.

I didn't think this was the best time to say so.

"Look, I know none of what happened here today is

your fault," I said. "But I have to know if you're okay with the Brannock party."

Faye seemed taken aback. "Of course. Why, of course. Don't worry about the party. Not for a minute. Cady will get with you on the menu and everything will be perfect. I promise."

Faye was definitely confident about handling the event, which made me breathe a little easier. She was the kind of person who would make things happen—no matter what.

I thanked her and headed toward the rear of the building where I'd parked my car. Just as I reached the receiving area, I heard someone call my name. I turned and saw Lourdes hurrying after me.

"I just wanted to make sure you're all right," Lourdes said, after she'd caught up with me.

Okay, that was nice of her—but weird, at the same time. Then I realized she had an ulterior motive.

Lourdes forced a smile. "You know, Faye has worked super hard to build the business. Cady is artistic, but it's Faye who makes this place run. If it weren't for her, Cady would still be baking cupcakes in her kitchen and selling them to whoever. So, please, don't hold this problem against Faye. Not because of Jeri, of all people. Okay?"

"We're good," I said. "I'll come back tomorrow and talk to Cady about the menu."

"Great," Lourdes said, and backed away. "Thanks."

I left the receiving area, jumped into my Honda and headed out, intent on finding a Starbucks, which I desperately needed. When I circled around to the front of the building, Jack Bishop popped into my head as I cruised through the parking lot toward the exit.

I'd seen him here when I arrived. Did he know he'd just missed a murder? That something huge had gone down and he'd driven away, totally oblivious?

For a few seconds I thought about calling him, telling him the whole story—except maybe for the part about that totally hot Detective Grayson—and flaunting the fact that, for once, my life was more cutting edge than his. But I was afraid he still might one-up me. I was in no mood.

I pulled out onto Ventura Boulevard, confident there had to be a Starbucks around here somewhere. I'd gone only a few blocks when I spotted the familiar green sign that always said "home" to me.

After I placed my order at the drive-thru, I pulled out my cell phone and saw that I had a message from Marcie. She absolutely loved the Flirtatious handbag I'd texted her about earlier and had already begun our usual three-pronged search mode—Internet, boutiques, and chain stores—to find one for each of us.

While I inched forward in line I called Kayla to get an update on what was going on at L.A. Affairs. She answered on the first ring.

"Oh my God, Haley, where are you?" she demanded.

I could tell immediately that she was in high-panic mode.

Jeez, I desperately needed that frappie now.

I eased up closer to the car in front of me.

"Edie and Priscilla are still behind closed doors," Kayla said.

"Still?"

"Still," Kayla said.

This was worse than I thought.

I leaned out my window. What the heck was taking that drive-thru guy so long?

"Eve found out that they are reviewing the caseloads of all the planners," Kayla said. "All of us."

Oh my God, if I didn't get my frappie soon, I might scream.

"That means any one of us could be let go," Kayla said.

Maybe I should abandon my car and go up on foot.

"They're probably looking for reasons to fire someone," Kayla said. "How are your events going? Is everything okay with them? Are there any serious problems?"

"No, nothing," I insisted. "I was just following up with the caterer at—"

Oh my God. *Oh my God.*

If anybody at L.A. Affairs learned about the murder at Cady Faye Catering today and there was bad publicity, I would be blamed. It had been my idea to hire them. I'd practically put the smack-down on Priscilla to let me use them for the Brannocks' St. Patrick's Day bash.

This could totally impact my probation period with L.A. Affairs. It could even get me fired, since Edie and Priscilla were in a management huddle and seemed anxious to cut someone loose.

Then another even worse thought hit me.

Oh crap.

What if things got totally out of control? L.A. Affairs' reputation could be ruined—everybody would lose their job if the company went under. Cady Faye's rep would take a major hit, too—they'd be lucky if they got to sell cupcakes out of Cady's kitchen to whoever.

Then, without even drinking my frappie, I knew exactly what I had to do.

I sat straight up in my seat. I was going to have to

solve this murder myself.   The line moved forward and I rolled up to the drive-thru window. The guy passed me my drink.

I passed it back and said, "Make it a venti."

* * *

"Have you heard anything?" Kayla murmured.

"No," I whispered back.

We were in the breakroom at L.A. Affairs the next morning making our usual let's-stall-as-long-as-possible cup of coffee. Apparently, the outcome of Edie and Priscilla's marathon meeting yesterday was still unknown.

I'm not big on suspense. If we didn't learn something soon, I was going to have to barge into their offices and ask them straight-out what was going on.

Kayla glanced over her shoulder, then whispered, "I heard they're considering shifting events around, reassigning them to different planners."

This couldn't be good.

"So they can fire someone?" I asked.

"Maybe. Or maybe not." Kayla leaned closer. "It could mean there's a huge event coming up, something prestigious. They want to make sure the planner they give it to isn't overbooked."

My spirits lifted. "So this could be good?"

Kayla nodded. "A successful A-list event can make your career here. Everybody wants to handle something high-profile."

My spirits lifted even further. This would be the perfect time for me to take on a big event and demonstrate my superior event planning skills, especially since my probation period wasn't up yet.

I'd managed to stay away from the office most of yesterday. Maybe I should stick around today and let Edie and Priscilla see how hard I'm working—even if it meant I'd have to actually work hard.

"I'll let you know if I hear anything more," Kayla said.

I dumped a few extra sugars into my coffee—just to celebrate the good news, of course—and headed for my office. I had a lot to do today so I started immediately by checking my Facebook page and making an appointment for a pedi. I logged onto my computer and spent a few minutes looking at the Macy's site, then ordered myself two sweaters and a pair of jeans. Just for the heck of it, I checked for the fabulous Flirtatious satchel but it was out of stock everywhere. I texted Marcie with the search update.

So far, my morning was rolling along pretty well, I decided as I sat back in my chair. Somehow, today I had to find a way to let Edie and Priscilla know what a fabulous planner I was so I'd have a shot at the hopefully-it's-true A-list event Kayla had speculated about. What better way to insure my continued employment?

A better way sprang into my head—solve Jeri's murder before word got out and reputations were ruined. Or mine, anyway.

In my experience it's always easier to find a murderer if there are suspects to choose from, and so far I had only two—well, one and a half, really.

The extra-large, giant leprechaun guy who'd taken off in the costume was at the top of my I-think-you-did-it list. All I needed to do was find out who he was. I dashed off a quick text to Wendy asking for the contact info for the two extra-large servers on her list.

My sort-of suspect was Lourdes. She'd made comments about not liking Jeri, which wasn't much to go on, but I had to start somewhere.

As long as I was stretching for suspects, I added Cady's name to my mental list. There had been some conflicting reports about whether or not she was actually on the premises when Jeri was killed, so I figured that was as good a reason as any to consider her a suspect.

My cell phone chimed and I saw I had a message from Wendy giving me the first names of the two extra-large servers, along with the explanation that Maisie's Costume Shop had no additional information because the guys didn't work for them. I sent her a thank-you reply.

I'd hoped she could give me all the info I needed, but no matter. I was, after all, a wannabe-semi-rock-star-detective and knew I could find their contact info somewhere.

Of course, this would be easier if I had a motive or maybe even some evidence. I was in good with Shuman, another LAPD homicide detective, and under normal circumstances I wouldn't hesitate to call him for inside info on the case. But I hadn't seen Shuman in a while—long story.

I knew there was no way I could pry anything out of Detective Elliston. Dan Grayson might be a different story—if he ever came to realize I wasn't a suspect, which didn't seem likely.

My office phone rang and I jumped out of my chair.

What if it was Edie and Priscilla calling me in to fire me?

What if it was Edie and Priscilla calling me in to assign mc a kick-ass cvcnt?

I grabbed the phone and heard, "Are you ready to

party?"

Good grief. It was Mindy, our receptionist. She was a nice enough person but she was forever getting things mixed up.

"Hello? Hello?" Mindy said. "Are you ready to party?"

"It's me. Haley," I said.

"Oh, jiminy, Haley," she said. "I hope you're not calling in sick today."

See what I mean?

"I'm in my office," I said. "You called me."

"I did? Oh, well, okay then, I guess you're ready to party, all right," Mindy said, and chuckled at her own joke.

"Did you need something from me?" I asked.

"What? Oh, yes. There's a man here to see you," she said. "His name is—oh, let me see what I wrote down. It's Don Brayman. No. It's Tom. Yes, Tom somebody. Erickson, maybe. Yes, it's Erickson. Tom Erickson—no, that's not it."

Mindy kept talking but I tuned out. I figured that sooner or later she'd be able to read her own handwriting—or I would just get up and walk to one of our interview rooms and see for myself who'd come to L.A. Affairs and asked for me specifically.

"—Dan Grayson." Mindy's voice cut through my thoughts. "Yes, it's definitely Dan Grayson."

I lurched out of my chair and slammed down the phone in one smooth Dancing-With-The-Stars move.

Detective Dan Grayson was here? At my office? He'd come to see me?

Oh my God. Was he going to arrest me?

No way was I going to stick around and find out.

I grabbed my handbag and three event portfolios, and

charged out of my office and down the hallway. I spotted Detective Grayson sitting in the interview room on my right. But I didn't stop, just paused long enough to say, "Sorry, I'm on my way out."

I turned on the speed—not easy in four-inch pumps, but luckily I have Mom's pageant legs—and passed the cube farm, the other interview rooms, Mindy's receptionist desk, and went out the door. The elevator was at the end of the hallway. A man was getting off.

"Hold the doors," I called.

I might have said that louder than I meant to.

The guy jumped out of the way as I ran inside. I jabbed the button for the parking garage six times.

Just as the doors slid closed, Dan Grayson charged out of L.A. Affairs.

Chapter 4

The elevator doors opened into the ground floor of the parking garage and—yikes!—there stood Dan Grayson. Oh my God, he'd run down the stairs and beat me here.

Wow, how hot was that?

He wasn't even breathing hard. I was—but that was only because I was afraid he'd arrest me. I swear.

"I need to talk to you, Miss Randolph," he said.

He was using his serious-cop voice. It was totally hot.

"Detective Grayson?" I asked, and squinted—yes, I actually did that—as if I didn't recognize him. "Was that you upstairs?"

He walked closer—wow, he was really tall—and gave me an are-you-kidding-me look.

I was in too deep to back out now.

"I don't usually see walk-ins. Next time you should make an appointment."

"I don't make appointments. I make arrests."

Oh, crap.

No way was I going to simply stand here and let him slap on the cuffs.

"I have several clients, important clients, very important clients, waiting for me," I said, as I hefted the event portfolios a little higher and backed away.

"Who?" he wanted to know, and gave me a let's-see

finger wave.

I had no idea which portfolios I'd grabbed in my mad dash out of the office.

"These are confidential," I said.

He rolled his eyes and yanked them out of my hand.

Damn, he was good.

Dan flipped open the top portfolio and read for a few seconds, then cut his gaze to me.

"Psychic readings? For *cats?*" he asked.

Okay, this was really embarrassing. But what could I do but push on?

"These cats are clients of Hollywood's most respected animal actor talent agent, and are preparing for a pivotal role in a major motion picture," I told him.

That was a total lie, of course. But it sounded better than admitting my clients were really over-indulged tweens in Calabasas, and I'd gotten stuck with the event after losing to Kayla in the best two-out-of-three in Rock Paper Scissors.

Dan raised an eyebrow and tilted his head at me. He wasn't buying it.

"Look," I said, "I don't come up with these crazy requests, I just plan the events I'm given."

I yanked my portfolios away from him and stomped off.

He was in front of me in two seconds, forcing me to stop. I glared up at him. He glared right back, then grinned.

Wow, what a grin.

I gave myself a mental shake. I had to keep my wits about me. Who knew why he was here and what he might be up to? Whatever it was, I figured it couldn't be good for me.

Still, his partner Detective Elliston wasn't with him—unless he was on a nearby rooftop coordinating the S.W.A.T team that was back-up for my arrest—so maybe something else was going on.

I made a show of huffing semi-irritably, straightening my shoulders and pushing my chin up, and said, "What can I do for you, Detective?"

Dan Grayson shuffled his feet a little, then shrugged.

"I wanted to let you know about your jacket," he said.

What the heck was he talking about?

"The one you had on yesterday when you pulled the victim out of the water," he said. "We took it into evidence."

This was the reason he'd scared the crap out of me? To let me know about my jacket I'd left hanging in the ladies room at Cady Faye to dry? Was this a supreme lame-o reason to come here, or what?

Was this some sort of cop subterfuge? Did he think he could lull me into an I'm-here-to-help-you conversation, then get me to confess to something?

I glanced around. Were there undercover cops in the garage shooting video of this meeting?

I fluffed my hair, just in case.

"So," he said, and blew out a heavy breath, "I, ah, I just wanted to let you know so you wouldn't think it had been stolen, or something."

He looked at me and I looked back. I couldn't think of anything to say and, apparently, neither could he. We seemed to be suspended in some sort of middle-school moment that neither of us wanted to break free of.

Finally, he seemed to give himself a little shake then said, "I'm not sure when it will be returned to you. At the conclusion of the case, whenever that happens."

"I don't want it back," I said. "It's got dead-person cooties on it."

Dan grinned. "Those are the worst kind."

I laughed. I couldn't help it. Something about Dan made me nervous and calm, all at the same time.

Still, I saw no reason not to turn this conversation into something that would benefit me.

"I didn't kill Jeri," I said.

He kept grinning, as if he'd expected I'd say that and would have been disappointed if I hadn't.

"I can't discuss the case," he said.

"I didn't ask you to discuss it," I told him. "I was simply telling you that I'm not the person you should be checking into."

Dan nodded. "And who do you think I should be investigating?"

Was he asking for my help? Was he hoping for some info I hadn't already divulged? Or, perhaps, had he uncovered no suspects and wondered if I had?

I didn't want to confess to my suspicion about Lourdes and Cady because, really, they were nothing but I'm-desperate-for-a-suspect thoughts. I figured that he already knew about the extra-large server who'd taken off without turning in his leprechaun costume, and I didn't want to look like an idiot by telling him something he already knew.

"I heard that Jeri wasn't well liked," I said.

He frowned a cop-frown. "Faye Delaney indicated she was highly regarded."

"By Faye, yes," I said. "But bosses are usually the last to know."

Dan nodded and was quiet for a while. "Did anyone mention that Jeri was romantically involved with someone?"

I knew immediately that if he was asking me this question it was because he'd found some indication that Jeri had been murdered by a psycho she'd been dating, or a jealous lover.

"Nobody said anything," I told him. "Did she have a boyfriend? Do you think he killed her?"

"Yes, and maybe," Dan said. "Her boyfriend was married."

Visions of a wronged wife with angry friends and relatives, and any ex-boyfriends that Jeri might have had, flashed in my head.

"Lots of people could have a motive for killing Jeri," I said.

Dan gave me a rueful smile. "And I'm checking out all of them."

I guess a homicide detective's work is never done.

"If I hear anything I'll let you know," I said.

"I would appreciate that," Dan said, and sounded as if he really meant it. He pulled a business card from his jacket pocket and passed it to me. "Call if you learn anything."

I took his card and headed for my Honda. He walked along with me, then hurried a few steps ahead to open the door for me.

I stood on one side, Dan on the other. Some sort of crazy heat circulated between us.

"Am I still not allowed to leave town?" I asked.

Dan leaned a little closer. He smelled great.

"I'd come after you, if you did," he said.

Wow. It might be fun to give it a try.

* * *

My cell phone chimed as I drove down Ventura Boulevard. When I stopped at the next light, I glanced at the screen and saw that it was a text message from Marcie recommending we put boots on the ground and do a hard-target search for the Flirtatious handbag tonight.

I was scheduled for a shift at Holt's this evening. I'd blown off working there last night using the touch-of-the-stomach-flu excuse—a personal favorite of mine. I saw no reason it couldn't stretch into a two-shift event.

Of course jeopardizing my job at Holt's, my sad-but-it's-true only reliable employer, might not have been the smartest move with this whole someone-could-get-fired thing going on at L.A. Affairs, but oh well. I texted Marcie back promising to meet her later tonight.

I had a number of events to follow up on, but the Brannocks' St. Patrick's Day party was the biggest in my windshield. It was just days away and I wasn't feeling all that great about Cady Faye Catering. Even though Faye had promised everything would be handled smoothly, I figured it wouldn't hurt to keep an eye on what was going on there.

Plus, now I had another suspect in Jeri's death. Detective Grayson had told me she was involved with a married man, a situation that offered a plethora of suspects. Maybe somebody who worked for Cady Faye Catering could give me some inside info on who the guy was, and how I could find him.

As I turned left from Ventura Boulevard into the shopping center's parking lot, Jack Bishop popped into my head. I'd seen him here yesterday. No sign of him today—so far, anyway. He could be super stealthy—as a way-hot private detective would be.

I cruised around to the rear of the building and parked. The space was jammed with cars, pick-ups, delivery trucks, and Cady Faye Catering vans. Just like yesterday, a van was backed into the receiving area. I grabbed my portfolio and went inside.

Nothing much had changed since yesterday. The catering staff formed an ant trail from somewhere deeper in the building to the van. Servers milled around getting into their Cady Faye vests and bow ties. Construction workers hustled back and forth, shouting and dragging equipment.

I found my way through the maze of hallways to the offices near the front of the building. Lourdes was inside one of them—a bare bones space crying out for a high-limit credit card from Macy's—working at her computer.

I'd considered her a suspect simply because she hadn't hesitated to let me know she didn't like Jeri. I wanted to get some info from her today that would make me move her into my mental yeah-you-probably-did-it category, or disregard her as a suspect completely.

"Hi," I called from the doorway. "Got a minute?"

Lourdes spotted me and said, "Sure, Haley. Come on in."

Lourdes' office was neat and orderly. File folders were stacked uniformly on the edge of her desk; her pencil cup, stapler, and paperclip holder were in perfect alignment with her keyboard.

"It looks like business as usual around here," I said, taking the chair in front of her desk.

"Of course," Lourdes said, squaring off her stapler. "We're extremely busy with multiple events every day. We can't let anything slow us down."

"Not even a murder?" I asked.

Okay, that sounded kind of stinky but I needed info and didn't have a lot of time to wait around for it.

Lourdes forced a smile. "I realize this might seem cold, but nothing can interfere with our work. Certainly not a personnel issue."

Finding an employee murdered seemed like more than a simple personnel issue, but I understood what Lourdes was getting at. Cady Faye Catering events were planned months in advance. Tons of preparation went into them—buying the food, preparing it, scheduling servers—and clients expected to get what they'd paid for, regardless.

"Are any of your employees weirded-out about Jeri getting killed here in the building?" I asked.

"Some," Lourdes said. "But nobody is worried there's a catering company employee murderer on the loose. Most of them let it roll off. They know Jeri was no saint."

"Because she was involved with a married man?" I asked.

"Not everybody is okay with that sort of thing," Lourdes told me.

I got the impression that Lourdes was one of those people who wasn't okay with it. I was one of those people also. I've got a thing about people being honest in their relationships.

Even though we'd broken up, Ty Cameron flashed in my head—that still happened a lot. When he'd been my official boyfriend, I'd been a real stickler about not getting involved—no matter how slightly—with anyone else.

Images of Ty lingered in my mind. I pushed hard to force them out.

"Jeri always did what she wanted to do with no

concern for anyone else," Lourdes said. She stopped, as if she thought she'd said too much, and gestured to the portfolio in my lap. "Are there any questions I can answer about the Brannock party?"

"I need to go over the menu with Cady," I said. "Is she here today?"

"Of course," Lourdes said. "She's in the kitchen."

Lourdes hadn't exactly been mega-forthcoming with info on Jeri, but there was still something she could help me with.

"One more thing," I said. "One of the size extra-large leprechaun costumes wasn't turned in. I need the contact info for the two guys who tried them on."

Lourdes hesitated, which didn't suit me, so what could I do but push ahead with a total lie?

"L.A. Affairs is responsible for the costumes," I said. "It's in our contract with the costume shop."

Lourdes stared at me. I could tell she didn't really believe me.

The important thing about telling a lie was to not oversell it. I sat there staring at Lourdes. I could almost see her brain working. Giving out confidential employee info could cause a problem, but offending me and possibly causing a dispute between L.A. Affairs and Maisie's Costume Shop—two places essential to the success of Cady Faye's Catering—would be a disaster.

Lourdes turned to her computer. "Names?"

I whipped out my cell phone and accessed Wendy's text, and showed it to Lourdes. She clicked a few keys, and a sheet of paper glided out of the printer. She passed it across the desk to me.

"Thank you," I said, tucking it inside the portfolio, and struggling to suppress my I-won smile.

I left her office. As I headed down the hallway, I spotted a young woman lingering nearby. She had on one of those white coats that a chef wears, and a funky red scarf covering her hair. I figured her for early twenties.

"Excuse me," she said quietly. "Is it okay if I talk to you?"

I stopped. "Sure."

She glanced back toward Lourdes' office. "Not here. Okay?"

I followed her around a corner, then another corner. We stopped near the janitor's closet. There wasn't a lot of action in this part of the building, so we had the place pretty much to ourselves—but maybe that was because a little farther down the hallway yellow crime scene tape covered the door to the ice room.

"My name is Sierra. I've worked here for a while," she said quietly. "Look, I know Lourdes has been talking crap about Jeri, and I wanted you to know it's not true."

"You and Jeri were friends?" I asked.

She gave me a sad smile. "We're in culinary school together. You know, the one in Pasadena. Faye's really good about giving students a chance. She hired me a few months ago, so I told Jeri she should apply here, too. She did, but it wasn't working out so well for her."

"Because Lourdes didn't like her?" I asked.

Sierra's shoulder sagged and she shook her head. "I guess I shouldn't have suggested it to Jeri. I knew Lourdes worked here but I didn't think she disliked Jeri so much. I swear I didn't."

"What happened?" I asked.

"Lourdes was struggling with some of her classes," Sierra said. "But, I mean, who wasn't? It's not as easy as people think."

"Hang on a second," I said. "Lourdes was in culinary school with you and Jeri?"

"Yes," she said. "Only Lourdes was having major money problems. She had to drop out. She kind of had it in for Jeri because Jeri was, you know, really great at everything, plus she got all kinds of scholarships that Lourdes thought she didn't really need. Lourdes thought it robbed her of the money she could have used to stay in school."

"So it must have really ticked her off when Faye hired Jeri to work here," I said.

"Like you wouldn't believe," Sierra said. "She seemed to think Jeri was angling for her job, trying to take over. It didn't help that Faye thought the world of Jeri."

I could understand how Lourdes must have felt. First, Jeri had been a stand-out in culinary school, eventually forcing her to drop out when Jeri got the scholarships Lourdes felt should have been hers. Then when she found a great job at Cady Faye, here comes Jeri, a darling in Faye's eyes.

"Despite what Lourdes says about her," Sierra said, "Jeri is—was—a good person."

"Even though she was involved with a married man?" I asked.

Okay, that was kind of crappy of me, but I wanted to get Sierra's read on that whole thing.

"They loved each other. Really," Sierra insisted. "He was getting a divorce. Jeri confirmed it with her roommate who worked for the attorney who was handling everything. Her name is Molly. The lawyer is that Horowitz guy whose face is plastered on all the buses. You can ask her yourself, if you don't believe me."

"So there's no chance this had anything to do with

Jeri's death?" I asked.

"No way," Sierra said.

"The guy she was involved with, he didn't change his mind? Didn't have a psycho wife? Kids who blamed Jeri for the breakup?" I asked.

Sierra shook her head. "They didn't have any kids. His wife was already involved with somebody else—they were getting a divorce before Jeri came along."

Damn. That pretty much destroyed my theory—and Detective Grayson's—that Jeri's death involved her married boyfriend.

"So who do you think killed Jeri?" I asked.

"There's only person here who didn't like Jeri," Sierra said. "Lourdes."

Chapter 5

Sierra went back to work and I stood outside the ice room for a few minutes thinking about what she'd told me. Lourdes, it seemed, had really disliked Jeri, maybe even hated her. But that situation had existed for a long time. Something major must have happened if Lourdes suddenly turned on Jeri and killed her.

I had no idea what it could have been.

I'd considered Cady a possible suspect also, since there was a question about her whereabouts during the time of the murder. But so far nobody had mentioned a problem between Cady and Jeri. Plus, Cady had had a serious melt-down when Lourdes had told her Jeri was dead.

My major suspect was the giant leprechaun who'd run away so quickly he'd made a mad dash out of here in a costume. Hopefully, I could come up with a motive when I found him.

I stared at the yellow tape crisscrossing the door to the ice room and thought about how Jeri had died. I'd seen a fresh scratch on her face, so obviously, there had been some sort of physical confrontation between her and her killer. Maybe it had started out small with an argument, then escalated. Things must have gotten crazy at that point because I'd seen that yucky dent in Jeri's skull.

Water had been pooled on the floor under the tank when I'd walked in and found Jeri, but there was no trail of water leading out the door. I wasn't sure how that was possible, except that maybe the murderer had come prepared with some sort of bag to put wet clothing in after the deed was done.

That made it premeditated. Whoever had done this to Jeri had put a lot of thought into it and had deliberately attacked, then drowned her.

A really ugly picture popped into my head. I didn't like it.

I started walking, following the sounds of the hammers, electric saws and drills, and loud voices of the construction workers, and found my way to the space that was being remodeled next door. A dozen or so men were busy doing all sorts of things with all sorts of tools and equipment. The front door and rear doors were propped open.

I knew the same thing was taking place on the other side of Cady Faye's. Faye had told me she'd tripled their business in the last year. They needed triple the space—which, to me, meant even more ways for the murderer to escape unnoticed by the constructions workers intent on doing their jobs.

Detective Grayson floated into my head. I wondered if he'd thought of these things, and figured that he must have. Still, it might be nice to compare notes with him—strictly in the line of duty, of course.

I turned around and headed back, then followed my nose to the kitchen. It was a big room crowded with stoves, ovens, sinks, prep tables, and other equipment. A dozen or so workers wearing hairnets and plastic gloves were elbow-to-elbow preparing food.

I spotted Cady seated at a desk wedged into a tiny office at the rear of the room, and walked over. The place was a mess. File folders, magazines, and papers were stacked on every flat surface. Clothing was piled in a chair, shoes underneath. Print-outs, notes, and schedules were pinned to a giant bulletin board. Cady was crouched over her desk reading something.

"Hi, Cady," I said.

She screamed—yes, actually screamed—and whirled around, throwing both arms in the air.

I noted that none of the workers came running, which made me think this wasn't an unusual occurrence.

"Oh, it's you," Cady declared. She clasped both hands against her chest and drew in several huge breaths.

"Sorry," I said, and stepped into the room.

"It's okay," Cady said, still heaving. "I'm fine. I'm fine."

"Really?" I asked.

Her gaze darted around the room, then landed on me.

"No, I'm not fine," she told me. "How could I be fine?"

Cady looked like she was going to lose it at any second.

I'm not good in that sort of situation.

"I wanted to discuss the menu for the Brannock party," I said. "But I can come back later."

"Oh, God," Cady said. She pushed her hands through her hair and gave herself a shake. "Let's do it now. Before Faye finds out and comes in here."

Cady rifled through the stacks on her desk, knocking several folders into the floor, then finally came up with a single sheet of paper.

"Green," she said, waving the paper in the air. "I'm making everything that's green. Spinach, asparagus, lettuce, mint, pistachio. Any kind of food you can think of that's green, I'm making it. And Irish. Irish beef stew, Irish soda bread, Irish corn chowder, Irish corned beef and cabbage. Green and Irish, green and Irish, green and Irish. I've got it, okay? Green and Irish."

Lourdes had described Cady as artistic—which, apparently, was code for a complete emotional wreck. I'd talked with Cady before and, while she'd seemed a bit scattered, she'd never been this crazed.

I caught the paper Cady was waving over her head and looked at it. It was the list of food Nadine Brannock had suggested that I'd given to Cady on my initial visit weeks ago to discuss the event. Cady hadn't expanded on anything or noted any comments on presentation. Not good.

Okay, now I was officially worried.

I knew expressing my concerns to Cady would be pointless, so I thanked her and headed for Faye's office. She was seated at her desk when I walked in.

The green duffel bag Wendy and I had found in the employee lounge yesterday was sitting in the corner by a tall file cabinet. I guess it hadn't been left behind, as I'd thought. I hadn't pegged Faye for a sexy lingerie and black lacy teddy kind of gal, but obviously, I was wrong.

"What's up with Cady?" I asked.

Faye looked lost. "I don't know what you mean."

"I need you to shoot me straight, Faye. A lot is on the line here. I just saw Cady. She's a mess. Does she need to see a doctor? Or maybe just go home until she can calm down?"

"Going home would serve no purpose," Faye said. "Cady doesn't have any children and that husband of hers would do more harm than good."

Her gaze darted to one of the photos on her desk.

Faye and Cady were posed side by side, flanked by two men. Their husbands, I figured.

"Let's just say that Harry Wills' primary interest in Cady is Cady Faye Catering," Faye said.

Lourdes had mentioned there was trouble in Cady's little corner of marital paradise, and it seemed that Faye's opinion of her brother-in-law Harry confirmed it. I glanced at the pictures of Faye's kids on her desk. Seemed family life had turned out very differently for the two sisters.

"Cady is really close to losing it," I said. "Is it because of Jeri's murder? Or is something else going on?"

"Oh, those detectives," Faye muttered and tossed the pen she was holding onto her desk. "They were here again this morning asking more questions. It upset her."

"Why were they asking Cady questions?" I asked.

"I have no idea. She wasn't even here with it happened," Faye said.

"Did she tell you what they wanted from her?" I asked.

"She wouldn't discuss it. Typical Cady. Refusing to face anything head on. This whole thing is ridiculous. Jeri's death was a tragic accident, not a murder."

"What makes you so sure?" I asked.

"Isn't it obvious?" Fay said. "Jeri went into the ice room looking for Cady, then somehow hit her head, fell into the water and drowned."

Apparently, the police hadn't told her about the scratches on Jeri's face and the dent in her skull.

I saw no need to get into it with her.

"And I'm positive that nobody—absolutely nobody—who works here would murder a co-worker," Faye said. "I don't run that kind of company."

"The police must have some sort of evidence," I pointed out.

"And I have evidence, too," Faye told me.

My senses jumped to high alert.

"Let me show you," Faye said, and grabbed a DVD out of her desk drawer. "Come with me."

I walked with her to the employee lounge. No one was inside. Faye switched on a television sitting on the counter that I hadn't noticed before, and slid the DVD into the player.

"It's the building's surveillance tape from the day of Jeri's death," Faye explained. "The landlord gave it to the detectives, but he kept a copy for himself. Insurance reasons, he said. He brought it here and insisted I watch it to prove that his complex is safe."

Faye pressed a button and the TV came alive with grainy black and white footage. It was a split-screen format, displaying views of the front and rear parking lots.

"Are these the only angles you have?" I asked.

"Some of the security cameras are off-line because of the construction," Faye said. She fast-forwarded the DVD. "This is shortly before Jeri died."

I glanced at the date and time stamp at the bottom of the screen, then studied the front parking lot. The stores in the shopping center formed a big "U" with parking spaces in the middle. The security camera that captured this footage must have been mounted near Cady Faye Catering because its field of view didn't show the caterer's storefront, the traffic lanes in front of it, or the first few rows of parking spaces, just a large area of the parking lot and a section of stores directly across from Cady Faye Catering.

The shopping center was busy. Lots of vehicles were

coming and going. People flowed in and out of the stores.

"There," Faye said, pointing at the television screen. "See that Mercedes? It's just like Cady's, which explains why someone thought she was here when she wasn't."

The film was too grainy to see the license plate, but it was definitely a light colored Mercedes.

"And look," Faye said. "There's another one."

Both of the cars were too far away to get a view of the driver and any passengers who might be inside, but Faye had a point—a Mercedes similar to Cady's in the parking lot wasn't unusual.

A line of vehicles followed the Mercedes. They moved into the frame as they drove down one of the aisles, circled to the next aisle, then disappeared out of the picture. My breath caught when I realized that one of the vehicles was a black Land Rover—Jack Bishop's Land Rover.

My heart did a little pitter-patter—that happens a lot where Jack is concerned—and it took a few seconds for me to focus on the screen again. Then it hit me—where was my car? I'd pulled into the parking lot as Jack was leaving. Why hadn't I seen myself in the footage? I realized then that the entrance/exit to the shopping center wasn't covered by the security camera.

I turned my attention to the other half of the split-screen and saw, a few minutes later, my Honda pull into the parking lot at the rear of the building. The angle of the camera caught only a portion of my car.

"There's a lot of the building and parking lot that isn't covered by the footage," I said.

"Just wait," Faye said. "You'll see what I'm talking about.

I did as she asked and watched the screen. Minutes

ticked by. At the rear of the building the Cady Faye Catering delivery van that had been backed up to the double doors drove away. Other cars pulled out. Vehicles kept rolling into the front lot, swinging into spaces. Shoppers made their way to the stores while others hoofed it to their cars, some carrying bags, got in, backed out, and drove away.

The security camera hadn't caught them, but black and white patrol units had pulled into the lot at some point, followed by a Crown Vic driven by Detectives Grayson and Elliston.

Jack Bishop's black Land Rover pulled into the front parking lot again. My heart did its usual pitter-patter—but for a different reason this time.

Jack had driven *back* to the shopping center? Why?

As I watched, he pulled into a space near the dry cleaners.

Okay, that was weird.

Of course, there could be a number of reasons why Jack would return to the shopping center. Maybe his dry cleaning hadn't been ready when he'd been in earlier. Maybe he'd forgotten something inside one of the stores he'd visited. Perhaps he was just looking for a spot to make a cell phone call.

Or perhaps he'd seen the flashing lights on the patrol cars and pulled in to see what was going down. Maybe he was just killing time. It didn't sound likely, but I guess even look-at-me-I'm-really-cool private detectives could have a slow day.

Another few minutes ticked by. Jack didn't get out of his Land Rover. Finally, he backed up and followed a gray Honda Pilot out of camera range.

I glanced at the date and time stamp on the screen and

realized that while Jack was sitting in the parking lot, I'd been waiting inside Cady Faye Catering to talk to the homicide detectives, only to have my eventual interview interrupted by Cady's arrival and the screaming fit she'd thrown upon learning about Jeri's death.

I realized, too, that the security camera hadn't caught her Mercedes as it had pulled into the parking lot.

"See?" Faye said. "Nothing unusual is going on."

"There isn't much on these tapes," I pointed out.

"Exactly," Faye declared. "If someone had actually murdered Jeri, wouldn't we see some sign of it outside? Somewhere on this footage? But there's nothing, no indication at all that a crime was committed."

I couldn't argue with that.

Faye gestured at the TV. "Nobody is running away. No cars are speeding off. No vehicles are racing through the parking lot—front or back. Nobody is jumping into a waiting car and tearing out of here."

There was also no sign of a giant leprechaun leaving the building.

"Everything is calm. Nobody is panicked," Faye said. She drew in a breath. "Which means there was no murder."

I thought that was a big leap to make, but Faye didn't give me a chance to say so.

"Those detectives are overzealous," she declared. "They're seeing a crime where one simply doesn't exist. And in the process they're threatening to damage the reputation of my company. I won't have it. Not after everything I've put into this place."

Faye popped the DVD out of the tray and switched off the television.

"Don't worry about Cady," she told me. "She will

have the food prepared for the Brannocks' party. Everything will be beautifully presented, delicious, and more than you or your clients could hope for."

Faye left and I stood there in the employee lounge thinking. A lot was going on in my head, but one thing was perfectly clear.

I had to talk to Jack Bishop.

Chapter 6

As soon as I got into my car outside of Cady Faye Catering I called Jack's cell phone. He didn't answer so I left a message asking him to call me right away. Then I pulled the paper from my portfolio that Lourdes had printed out for me with the contact info for the two extra-large servers, picked one of them, and punched his address into my cell phone.

GPS took me to the 101 freeway. I headed east, then transitioned south onto the 405 and exited on Sunset Boulevard toward UCLA. Many apartment buildings surrounded the campus. I found the one where extra-large, possible-costume-thief-and-murderer Colby Harmon lived off Hilgard Avenue, and squeezed my Honda into a spot at the curb.

Like everything else in the area, the building was well maintained and surrounded by palm trees, shrubbery, and flowering plants. It looked great—on the outside. Since I suspected the building was occupied mostly by students, I doubted the interior would be as nice.

I followed the signs around the building, went through a door that had been propped open, and found apartment 112. The place had a barebones, industrial look to it. Music pounded from behind a closed door and voices floated down the stairwell from the upper floors. Something in here didn't smell so great.

I knocked on Colby's door. It opened right away.

"Hey! How's it going?" he greeted.

Colby was extra-large, all right. Tall, blonde, big shoulders, early twenties, and kind of cute. He had on a stretched-out T-shirt and shorts, and was holding a beer.

On the drive over I'd thought about how to play this and had come up with a couple of scenarios. After all, this guy was possibly a murderer, one of my definite he-probably-did-it suspects. I had to be ready for anything.

But seeing Colby leaning against the door giving me a goofy life-is-great smile, I decided to take the most direct route.

"I'm here to pick up the costume," I said.

"Well, hey, great! Come on in!" Colby stepped back and swung the door open wide.

Wow, could it be this easy? Colby seemed very cooperative—and a little drunk—so I was sure I could get any information out of him that I wanted, namely a confession to Jeri's murder. I envisioned myself giving Dan Grayson a phone call and announcing that I'd solved the case.

Cool.

I walked inside. From the tiny entryway I could see the living room. It was cluttered with pizza boxes, take-out cartons, paper plates, fast-food bags and wrappers, and beer cans.

Something smelled really bad in here.

"Where's the costume?" I asked, since I wasn't all that excited about searching the place.

"What costume?" Colby asked, and tipped up his beer.

"The leprechaun costume," I said. "The one from Maisie's Costume Shop you wore when you left Cady

Faye Catering."

Colby frowned, as if he were thinking hard, then said, "Want a beer?"

"No," I said.

"Okay, come on in the kitchen."

Good grief.

I followed as Colby ambled down the short hallway into the kitchen. Yikes! The trashcan overflowed and the sink was filled with dirty dishes. Something really creepy looking was crusted on the stove and counter tops.

Colby opened the fridge—I didn't dare look inside— studied it for a while, then turned back to me and said, "Hey. Want a beer?"

"Look, I'm here to get the costume," I told him. "The leprechaun costume you stole from Cady Faye Catering yesterday."

Colby frowned again and squeezed his eyes shut, causing him to sway for a bit, then he looked at me again.

"A leprechaun costume? I stole a leprechaun costume?" He threw back his head and laughed. "That's killer, man. Hey, I can wear it to a St. Patrick's Day party, huh? Do I—do I really have a leprechaun costume?"

I was beginning to doubt it.

Suddenly, the next name on Lourdes' printout looked very promising. I headed for the door.

"Hey, want a beer?" Colby called.

* * *

His name was Tanner Stephens and he lived in one of Sherman Oaks' less desirable apartment complexes. I found the location easily enough, parked and went inside. The building retained its weren't-the-'80s-great vibe, but it was clean and quiet.

I found his apartment on the second floor and rang the doorbell. Nobody answered so I rang it again. Eventually, I heard muffled noises from inside, and the door opened slowly. An extra-large guy with close-cropped brown hair, dressed in jeans and a white T-shirt, looked out at me. I figured him for mid-twenties.

"Tanner Stephens?" I asked.

He glanced up and down the hallway, then looked at me.

"That's me," he said quietly.

Okay, he looked like a nice guy, but he definitely seemed weirded-out. Was it because he'd killed Jeri?

I should be so lucky. Once more I flashed on calling Detective Grayson and making him leprechaun-green with envy that I'd solved the case before he did.

"I'm here to pick up the costume," I said.

Tanner drew back a little. "They really sent somebody for it?"

Oh my God. This guy had the costume. Had I found my murder suspect?

My heart beat a little faster. I didn't want to spook him and have him run off before I got to call Dan and gloat. I forced myself to play it cool.

"Haley Randolph. I'm the costume police."

I did look very official in my awesome black business suit I'd expertly complemented with white and gray accessories, and teamed with a no-nonsense black-and-white checked Kate Spade satchel.

"I can explain," he said. "I just—wait, come inside."

Tanner stood back and I walked in. I didn't feel so great about going into the apartment of a possible murderer, but what choice did I have?

His place was small and decorated with what looked like yard sale treasures. The living room held a futon, a couple of chairs, crates that served as bookshelves, and a big computer desk.

Nothing smelled funny.

"Please, sit down," he said, motioning me toward a futon.

I sat and he dropped next to me.

"I admit I took the costume," he said. "But I wasn't stealing it. Why would I want a leprechaun costume?"

He had a point.

"Look, I had to get out of there," Tanner said. "As soon as I heard that girl had been found dead, I had to take off."

My senses jumped to high alert. Was Tanner about to confess?

Mentally, I rehearsed my I-solved-the-murder chant for Dan and his partner, and considered adding a Snoopy happy dance and a booty-pop or two.

"Did you kill her?" I asked.

"No," Tanner said. He pulled back and looked stunned. "No. God, no. I didn't kill her. I didn't even know her."

"You have to admit that taking off dressed in a leprechaun costume makes you look guilty," I pointed out.

He nodded. "Yes, I realize that. But you have to see it from my point of view. I'm almost finished with school and I'm trying to get a job at JPL, the Jet Propulsion Lab near Pasadena. I'll need a security clearance. I couldn't take a chance that hanging around, getting questioned by the police might screw that up, somehow."

I definitely understood his problem, but I wasn't willing to let it go so quickly.

"Did you have anything to do with Jeri's death?" I asked.

He shook his head. "I work all kind of jobs. Anything, really, to bring in some money. I've worked for that catering company a couple of times, setting up, serving food, bartending sometimes. But I don't really know anybody there."

He sounded sincere and his story made sense. I believed him.

"Did you see anything suspicious going on?" I asked.

Tanner thought for a couple of seconds, then said, "Nothing unusual."

"Have the police contacted you?" I asked.

"No," Tanner said. "I figured they might track me down, somehow, but they haven't shown up. Just you."

It was kind of cool knowing I'd tracked down a lead that the detectives had missed. For a few seconds I considered telling them—just for the sake of full disclosure and not because I wanted to throw it in their faces, of course—then decided that I didn't want to be responsible for blowing Tanner's big chance at a job at JPL.

I headed for the door.

"Do you want the costume?" Tanner asked.

"Wear it to the event," I said, and left.

* * *

As soon as I arrived at L.A. Affairs and walked down the hallway toward my office, I spotted Kayla. Her gaze homed in on me like a couple of line-of-sight laser beams.

"Run!" she exclaimed.

I went into total panic mode.

Oh my God, were Detectives Elliston and Grayson here? Were they waiting for me? Did they intend to arrest me?

Kayla rushed to me, grabbed my arm, and pulled me into the photocopy room. She slammed the door and fell back against it.

"You've got to keep out of sight," she told me, in a low voice. "Don't let Edie and Priscilla know you're in the office."

I went into total double-panic mode.

Edie and Priscilla must have finished their review of each planner's workload and decided to let someone go—and it was me. Oh my God, they were going to fire me?

Kayla opened the door a crack, peeked out, then turned to me again.

"It's worse than we thought," she said.

Yikes! Did that mean Edie and Priscilla had decided to fire several people?

"It's the Daughters of the Southland," Kayla told me.

Okay, now I was really confused.

"Who are they?" I asked.

"Some organization of old ladies who like to make everybody's life miserable. Every year they come to us to plan their annual luncheon," Kayla said, her voice rising slightly. "And they're horrible. Terrible. Absolutely awful."

She must have read my what-the-heck-look because she kept talking.

"The Daughters of the Southland are old. I mean, really old, like in their fifties and sixties—some of them are even older," Kayla said. "And every one of them is cranky and crabby. They can't agree on anything. They're always changing their minds, calling us, wanting this, wanting that. Then, another one of them will call and insist on something totally different. They bicker and argue and make life hell for whoever is planning their event. It's so bad nobody here wants to work with them."

"That's what Edie and Priscilla have been doing behind closed doors?" I asked.

"Yes," Kayla said. "They know none of us can stand to be in the same room with those crazy old ladies, so now they're forcing somebody to take on the event."

Oh my God. This was almost worse than thinking Edie and Priscilla were going to fire me—or that Detectives Elliston and Grayson were going to arrest me.

"Who are they assigning the event to?" I asked.

"I haven't heard," Kayla said. "Just try to avoid Edie and Priscilla."

"No problem," I said.

Kayla opened the door, checked the hallway, and we both hurried to our offices.

Since I didn't want to run the risk that Edie or Priscilla might spot me in the hallway or breakroom and assign me to that dreadful event, I was forced to stay in my office and do actual work.

I still hadn't heard back from Jack Bishop. I needed to find out why I'd seen his Land Rover in the surveillance video outside Cady Faye Catering twice, around the time of Jeri's murder. Of course, I knew there could be a perfectly innocent reason or perhaps just a coincidence, but I doubted it. I called him again and left another message.

The afternoon dragged on. I only got through it by focusing on meeting tonight with Marcie at The Grove, one of our favorite shopping centers, to hunt down the new Flirtatious satchel. Shortly before my official quitting time—okay, really it was 45 minutes early—I shifted into stealth-mode and left the office undetected.

On the drive, I couldn't help thinking that with the two extra-large servers off my list, I was getting low on murder suspects. I pulled into the parking garage and circled up to the third level, then swung into a spot near the elevators.

Marcie was going to meet me at Nordstrom, but I wanted to take another shot at talking to Jack Bishop before we began our Flirtatious search. I walked to a railing that overlooked shopping center, pulled out my phone and called Jack.

The view from this spot was awesome. The sun was setting, painting the sky in a dozen shades of gray and blue. In the distance were high-rise office buildings. Stretched out to my right were shops and stores, and immediately below me was an Italian restaurant's second-story balcony. A few tables were set up in the secluded dining area and were covered with snowy white linens; china and crystal sparkled beneath the twinkle lights.

Only one table was occupied. A man sat there alone, though the table was set for two. He had on a dark suit. His hair was a light brown. Even though he was seated I could tell he was tall with an athletic build.

From my angle above him I couldn't see his face but something about him looked familiar. He drummed his fingers on the table, shifted in his chair, pushed his hand through his hair, then—

My heart slammed against my ribs.

Oh my God. It was Ty, my official—former—official boyfriend.

I swayed against the railing. We'd broken up and it was over between us. Really. We'd seen each other only a couple of times, and it hadn't gone well, but still.

An image flashed in my head, taking my breath away: what if he was sitting at the table waiting for his date to show up?

I didn't know how I'd bear to see him jump up from his seat as she approached, greet her, probably kiss her. My whole body ached at the thought.

No way could I stand here and watch that happen.

I turned to go, then saw Ty rise from his chair. A man approached. They shook hands, then sat down.

Business, I realized. It was only a business meeting.

Marcie always said she doubted things would ever be over between Ty and me. I hadn't believed her.

But maybe, just maybe, she was right.

Chapter 7

As I headed through the parking garage toward the elevators the next morning, my cell phone rang. Kayla's name appeared on the caller I.D. screen.

Not a great way to start my day.

A phone call from Kayla when I was only minutes from arriving at L.A. Affairs could only mean that something major had gone down this morning—already.

Jeez, what now?

Really, I had enough on my mind. That whole thing with seeing Ty last night at The Grove was still bouncing around in my head. I'd told Marcie about it—as a BFF would—and she'd been sympathetic and understanding. She'd also told me that Ty and I would probably never be done with each other—which was also something a BFF would do, only this time it was kind of annoying.

I didn't want her to be right.

Our evening had ended on a high note when we'd gone into Nordstrom and—yahoo!—found that a friend of Marcie's had just gotten a sales clerk job there. She'd confided that another shipment of the totally awesome Flirtatious satchel was expected in a day or so, and promised to hold back two of them for Marcie and me—making her, of course, our new BFF.

I was tempted to ignore my ringing cell phone—it's hard to face a problem before my first cup of breakroom coffee—but Kayla wouldn't be calling me so early if it weren't important. I hit the green button and answered.

"Something major is going down," Kayla said in a low voice.

I pictured her crouched under her desk, cupping her hand over her phone.

"I just heard that Edie and Priscilla have decided who's going to handle the annual luncheon for the Daughters of the Southland," Kayla whispered.

"Is it me?" I asked.

Okay, I guess it was kind of crappy to think of myself first but, jeez, it was early.

"I don't know," Kayla said. "I'm telling you, Haley, working with these grouchy, cantankerous old women is a death sentence. You'll end up as gray-haired and wrinkled as they are."

That wasn't a look I was going for.

"If Edie and Priscilla stick you with this event, you can still try to get out of doing it—and you should," Kayla said.

I wasn't worried. I have excellent I-can-get-out-of-anything skills.

"Thanks for the heads-up," I said, and ended the call.

Just as I was about to drop my phone into my handbag—a Gucci tote I'd paired with my killer gray suit and crisp white accessories—it rang again. Jack Bishop's name flashed on the screen.

I wasn't in the best mood this morning—thanks to that whole Ty thing and those horrible Daughters of the Whatever that Edie and Priscilla might try to stick me with—and it kind of annoyed me that he'd taken so long to get back to me—which wasn't reasonable but there it was.

"Where have you been?" I barked, when I answered the phone.

"Miss me?" Jack asked.

Oh my God, he was using his Barry White voice. I'm totally helpless against his Barry White voice.

Still, I pushed on.

"You might want to start returning your calls," I told him. "You could want a call-back one day when you need to find me for something."

"I can always find you," Jack said.

He sounded so sure of himself—which was totally hot, of course—but it annoyed me.

"Yeah?" I asked. "Like you're such a fabulous detective?"

"Turn around."

Oh, crap.

I whirled around and spotted Jack leaning against a support pillar, looking awesome in jeans, CAT boots, and a black polo shirt—and way too sure of himself.

He walked toward me and tucked away his cell phone with a casual flip of his wrist. He was early thirties, tall with dark hair, a good build, and a killer grin.

I melted a little—but, jeez, I hadn't had my first cup of coffee yet.

Anyone in my position would have done the same thing.

"So what's up?" he asked, stopping in front of me.

It took me a few seconds to recall why I'd thrown a kind-of-sort-of fit about trying to contact him, and I finally said, "What were you doing cruising through that shopping center on Ventura two days ago?"

"You were following me?" Jack grinned.

Like I could be such a good P.I. he wouldn't know I was tailing him. Something to shoot for, I guess.

"I was at Cady Faye Catering," I said. "I'm

coordinating a St. Patrick's Day party for a Hollywood couple, the Brannocks. Cady Faye is handling the food."

Jack tilted his head. "You were desperate to contact me so you could hand-deliver my invitation?"

"What were you doing there?" I asked.

Jack shrugged. "Working a case. A rather nasty divorce."

I resisted the urge to do a nah-nah-nah-I'm-working-a-murder, and said, "You were following someone?"

"My client suspects her husband is involved with another woman. I was confirming it for her," Jack said.

Jeri's married boyfriend popped into my head and, for a few seconds, I wondered if it was his wife who'd hired Jack. Then I remembered that Sierra had told me the soon-to-be ex-wife was already involved with someone else. Still, she could have had a change of heart.

"Does your case involve Jeri Sutton?" I asked.

Jack wouldn't easily give up info in an investigation, but I knew he'd tell me if it were important.

"Jeri was killed inside Cady Faye Catering," I said. "I saw your Land Rover on the surveillance video."

Jack tensed. "You're not investigating the case, are you?"

His chest puffed out and his shoulders squared, so I figured he already knew I was involved. But no way was I getting into it with him—not this early in the morning—so what could I do but lie?

"No," I insisted.

His eyes narrowed, as if he thought I wasn't telling the truth, so what could I do but amp up my lie?

"The employees at Cady Faye are worried about their safety," I said. "I thought maybe you saw something when you were in the parking lot."

Jack's gaze lingered on me for a few more seconds—but not in a good way—and finally he said, "What happened?"

I gave him a rundown of what I knew, leaving out everything about how I was actually investigating the murder.

Jack shook his head. "There's no connection with your murder victim."

"But the guy you were following was cheating?" I asked.

"He was cheating," Jack said.

I'd hoped for a red hot lead that would take me to Jeri's murderer but it seemed that another of my theories had fizzled.

"Stay out of this," Jack told me.

I didn't promise that I would—Jack wouldn't have believed me anyway. I said good-bye and took the elevator up to L.A. Affairs.

The office was unusually quiet—I guess all the planners were lying low, afraid Edie or Priscilla would capture them in the hallway and give them that dreadful event to handle—so I went to the breakroom. No one else was there. I made myself a cup of coffee—which took no time at all, oddly enough—and went to my office.

I was disappointed that Jack hadn't been any help with my investigation into Jeri's murder, but I still had another source of information I could turn to.

Sierra, who worked at Cady Faye Catering and had been in culinary school with both Jeri and Lourdes, had told me that an attorney named Horowitz was handling the divorce of Jeri's married boyfriend, and that Jeri's roommate who worked in his office could confirm everything. Since I didn't have much else to go on, I decided to check her out.

I spent a couple of hours doing some actual work, then looked up the attorney on the Internet, gathered my things and headed out.

* * *

The office of attorney Rowland Horowitz was located on Alameda Avenue in Burbank. It was an older, one-story stucco building that looked as if it had been there for a while. I parked in the rear and went inside.

The reception area was small with hardwood floors, nice furniture, a year's worth of magazines on a side table, and a little glass window where the receptionist sat. Nobody was waiting. The place was silent. I figured most everybody was out for lunch.

Sierra had told me that Jeri's roommate was named Molly. The girl behind the glass could definitely have been a Molly. She was about my age, with red hair she'd styled in a ponytail.

She looked like an open, honest person, not someone who'd hold back the info I was after concerning Jeri's married boyfriend who, hopefully, had a psycho wife that might have attacked and killed Jeri.

I mean that in the nicest way.

"Hi," I said, and introduced myself as I approached the window. "Are you Molly? Sierra said I should talk to you. It's about Jeri."

She gasped and pressed her palms to her cheeks.

"I can't believe that happened to Jeri. Getting killed like that, at the place she loved," she whispered. "She was so nice. I mean, really nice. The best roommate ever."

"Everybody says that about Jeri," I agreed. "Well, except for some people at the catering company."

Molly frowned. "I know. That one girl there, what was her name, Lourdes? Jeri told me all about her."

"Some people were talking crap about Jeri because her boyfriend was still married," I said.

"They shouldn't say those things about Jeri and him," Molly told me. "He was definitely getting a divorce—not that he wanted one, to start with. His wife was cheating on him. But he was totally onboard with ending it. Mr. Horowitz is handling the whole thing."

"So there wasn't a future ex-wife in the picture who might have had it in for Jeri?" I asked.

Molly gasped and her eyes widened. "No way. Absolutely not. "

Okay, so my theory hadn't panned out

"I can't believe people are saying those things." Molly seemed angry now. "Well, fine. If the place goes out of business like Jeri thought it might, I guess they have it coming."

According to Fay, business had tripled in the last year. I'd seen for myself that they were expanding into the two storefronts that bordered their current location.

Still, an oh-no vibe shook me. If Cady Faye Catering went under, they'd better hang on long enough to complete my St. Patrick's Day party for the Brannocks or I'd be in major trouble.

"Why would Jeri think Cady Faye would go out of business?" I asked.

Molly pressed her lips together and her cheeks turned pink. "Oh, well, you know, there were problems—but every place has problems. Right?"

That was a lame answer. But I figured Molly had

decided she'd said enough so I didn't push it. I'd gotten the information I'd come here for—even if it wasn't all that helpful in finding a killer.

"So, you need a divorce, too?" she asked.

Her question took me surprise, though it would have been a great cover for coming here to talk to her.

Wish I'd thought of it.

"Me?" I asked. "No."

"Oh, I just thought that since you knew about Jeri and everything that was going on at the catering company with—" Molly stopped. "Well, never mind. Sorry. Listen, I've got to get back to work."

"Sure," I said.

I left the office and headed for my car with the distinct feeling that Molly had been holding back on me. But was it something important?

I couldn't be sure.

Chapter 8

"It's all b.s.," Bella mumbled. "You ask me, it's nothing but b.s."

"What's b.s.?" I asked, though I was more focused on the latest issue of *People* I was flipping through.

We were seated in the breakroom of Holt's Department Store. So far Bella and I had stretched our fifteen-minute break to twenty minutes—nice, but nowhere near our record.

Other employees came in, chatting, heating their food in the microwave or getting a snack from the vending machine. Someone had decorated the place with paper leprechauns, pots of gold, rainbows, and Irish flags.

I'd blown off my shifts at Holt's for the last two nights, but couldn't do it again. Sad as it was, I needed this job—at least until my probation was up at L.A. Affairs.

"All of it," Bella said. "All of it is nothing but b.s."

Bella—coffee to my vanilla—had been talking for a while now about something. I wasn't sure what, exactly, because I'd drifted off. This in no way affected our status as BFFs at Holt's. We'd worked together long enough to understand each other, as only BFFs can.

I'd picked up a word or two in her rant about the price of getting a good education. Bella intended to be a hairdresser to the stars and was working here to save for beauty school. In the meantime, she practiced on herself. Tonight, in what I could only think was an ode to the Irish,

77

she'd fashioned her hair into the shape of a shamrock atop her head.

The breakroom door swung open and Sandy, another of my BFFs here at Holt's, walked in. Sandy was about my age, blonde, really cute, and had a boyfriend who should have been smothered at birth. She met him on the Internet and he routinely treated her like crap, something everyone but Sandy could easily see.

"Hey, how's it going?" Sandy said, getting a soda from the vending machine. She sat down at the table with us. "Can one of you give me a ride home tonight?"

"Something happen to your car?" Bella asked.

"No, my car is great," Sandy said. "My boyfriend's car broke down."

"I'm not taking that dirt bag anywhere," Bella told her.

"Dump him," I said, for about the millionth time. "He's a loser."

"He isn't a loser," Sandy said. "He's an artist."

"He does tattoos," I said.

"That's art, Haley," she insisted. "Anyway, we're kind of in limbo right now."

"Let me guess," Bella said. "That's *his* idea."

"Well, yeah," Sandy admitted. "Last night he called me because his car broke down and he wanted me to pick him up."

"So I guess you dropped everything and ran to get him?" I asked.

"I had to," Sandy said. "He was with someone and she had to get to work."

"*She?*" Bella's eyes bugged out. "He was out with another girl and he called *you* to pick them up?"

"And you *did it*?" I asked.

"Well, she had to get to work," Sandy pointed out. "But he says that just proves how much he cares for me."

"What the hell are you talking about?" Bella asked.

Honestly, I was lost here, too.

Sandy seemed clear on everything, however, and said, "Don't you see? He lied to that other girl about being involved with someone else—me. But he told me the truth. He didn't even make up a big story or anything— like she was his cousin, or something—when I picked them up. He says that just proves he holds me in a much higher regard than her."

"Lord have mercy," Bella moaned, shaking her head.

"So why do you need a ride home tonight?" I asked,

"Because he needs my car," Sandy said.

"But he couldn't pick you up after work?" I asked.

"He has a date," Sandy said.

"I'm out of here." Bella headed for the door.

I was about to sprint out behind her when the door swung open and Rita, the cashiers' supervisor, stormed in. She was about as wide as she was tall, and always wore stretch pants and a shirt with a farm animal on it. Tonight, it was a cow being ridden by a leprechaun.

"Break time is over, princess," she barked at me.

I hated Rita. In fact, I double-hated her, triple-hated her, and now simply hated her to infinity.

I'm pretty sure she felt the same way about me.

I got up and dumped my trash, then walked out of the breakroom without so much as a glimpse in her direction.

My little corner of retail purgatory tonight was the housewares department. I was okay working there because I could slip into the stockroom often, pretending to look for something for a customer.

I mean, really, just because you had a job, did that

mean you had to actually work? Personally, I saw little correlation between the two.

I spotted an old couple near the pots and pans looking confused, as if they needed help, and my own brand of customer service immediately took over. I whipped around to head in the opposite direction and ran smack into someone.

Yikes! I jumped back, then looked up.

Oh, crap.

It was Detective Dan Grayson

How had he sneaked up on me like that? I have excellent avoidance skills. Was he really stealthier than me? Jeez, how annoying.

Then it hit me—why was he here? Whatever the reason, I figured it couldn't be good for me.

"I can't talk now," I told him in what I hoped was my most serious I'm-dedicated-to-my-job voice.

I guess I didn't pull it off very well because he shifted closer and said, "What I have to say won't take long."

I hoped his short statement wouldn't include the words "under" and "arrest."

"I understand you're working for the costume police," Dan said.

Oh, crap. That's the stupid excuse I'd given those extra-large guys when I'd gone to question them about Jeri's murder.

Still, I wasn't going to stand here and let Dan Grayson get the upper hand. I gazed up at him trying for a combined look of innocence and nonchalance—which would have been a heck of a lot easier if he didn't have those gorgeous blue eyes—but he seemed totally immune.

Damn. I hate it when that happens.

"What were you doing questioning a suspect?" he

asked. He held up his hand to silence me as if he thought I'd deny it, which was true but insulting just the same. "I talked to them both a few minutes ago. They told me you were there."

"What took you so long?" I asked. "I was on to that lead ages ago."

I'd hoped to distract him from discussing my involvement in Jeri's investigation, but he wasn't having it.

"On the day of the murder," Dan said, "did you see Cady Wills arrive at the catering company?"

Okay, this was a totally lame thing to ask me. He knew very well that I'd seen Cady's arrival because he was there when she'd walked in and had a total meltdown after Lourdes told her about Jeri.

"I saw her come in at the same time you did," I told him.

"Not before?" he asked.

Okay, now I got it.

"Several people had mentioned they thought they'd seen Cady earlier," I said. "But I didn't see her."

Dan nodded and, for some reason, I felt disappointed that I hadn't come up with some fabulous new info that would break the case wide open for him.

I wished I had a lead or some evidence to share with him, but I didn't. Everything I'd turned up so far had gone nowhere. All I had was suspicion and some unrelated loose ends.

"Have you uncovered anything," Dan asked, and gave me a little grin, "in your job as the costume police?"

I grinned back—I couldn't help it. He had one of those grins.

"Nothing," I said. "How about you? Want to share

something?"

His grin morphed into something totally different, and I got the impression he wasn't thinking about Jeri's homicide investigation.

It made me forget about the case, too.

He was giving off an I'm-going-to-ask-you-out vibe—which, hopefully, I wasn't confusing with an I-still-think-you-might-be-a-suspect vibe—but he didn't say anything. We shared a long, smoldering middle-school moment, then both of us seemed to come to our senses at the same time.

"Maybe when this case is closed?" Dan asked.

"Maybe," I said.

He gave me another little sideways grin which, in turn, caused my heart to do a weird little skip. But when he walked away I wasn't thinking about my erratic heartbeat. I was thinking about Cady.

Apparently, Dan considered her a suspect in Jeri's death.

But why?

* * *

"Something major just went down," Kayla told me. "Have you heard?"

I hadn't but, of course, I wanted to—but only if it was something good, which I doubted, given the way my week had gone so far.

We were walking through the hallway at L.A. Affairs. I'd just arrived—a few minutes late but oh well—and was headed for a rendezvous with a desperately needed first cup of coffee in the breakroom. Kayla, who always got there early, seemed wired already.

"Priscilla assigned the Daughters of the Southland luncheon this morning first thing," Kayla said. "She hired a new girl and stuck her with it."

I was in no mood to be toyed with.

"Are you sure?" I asked.

"Positive," Kayla told me. She heaved a sigh of relief. "Looks like we're in the clear."

She headed back the other way and I kept walking toward the breakroom.

This was definitely good news—on a day when I could use some. The Brannocks' St. Patrick's Day party was this evening. Everything was pretty much done—I'm actually darn good at this job—but there were always a few last minute things to handle and, of course, a snag or two to deal with. Today's possible snag was Cady Faye Catering.

"Haley?"

I heard Priscilla call my name as I passed her office. My Holt's training immediately took over. I found another gear and walked faster.

"Haley?" she called again. "Haley!"

There was really no place I could escape Priscilla—this works much better when there's a stockroom to hide in—so I stopped and turned around, as if I hadn't heard her call my name three times already.

Priscilla hurried toward me looking a bit grim. I flashed on the possibility that Kayla had been wrong and that Priscilla was about to assign the Daughter of Southland's luncheon to me. Immediately, I mustered my I-can-get-out-of-this brain cells—not easy without the benefit of a mocha frappuccino from Starbucks, a Snickers bar, or a cup of coffee.

"I need to check with you about the Brannock party

today," Priscilla said, in a low voice. "Is Cady Faye Catering handling everything to our standards?"

Yikes! This might be worse than getting stuck with that dreadful old ladies' luncheon. I'd convinced Priscilla to let me use Cady Faye. No way did I want her to know I was worried about their work—not with my probation period nearly over.

"Great," I lied—what else could I do? "Everything is great."

"Excellent." Priscilla smiled. "Now that I have your recommendation, I'm going to let all the other planners know Cady Faye Catering is on our list of approved vendors. I'll announce it at our next weekly office meeting—and I'll let everyone know you discovered them."

Oh, crap.

"Keep up the good work, Haley," Priscilla said, and headed back down the hallway.

If Cady Faye Catering screwed up this event today it would look bad, really bad, on me. I couldn't let that happen. I grabbed the Brannocks' portfolio out of my office and left.

Chapter 9

Of course, the food for the Brannock's party wasn't my only problem. Jeri had been murdered at the Cady Faye Catering location, which meant there was a good possibility that somebody who worked for the company had killed her—and that person just might also be working at the Brannocks' party tonight.

I hit the Starbucks drive-thru closest to the L.A. Affairs office and powered up my brain cells with a mocha frappuccino, then headed toward Cady Faye Catering on Ventura Boulevard.

The biggest thought screaming in my head was that if something went down at the Brannocks' tonight, L.A. Affairs' reputation would be ruined—to say nothing of my chances of continued employment.

I sipped my frappie and wondered if maybe there really was some psycho, catering-company-server killer on the loose who would do away with another Cady Faye employee tonight. It didn't seem likely, but my investigation into Jeri's death hadn't turned up anything solid. Detectives Elliston and Grayson hadn't made an arrest so, apparently, they weren't doing any better than I was.

The one crucial piece of this whole thing that was still missing was motive. Who would want to kill Jeri?

Lourdes was the only person I'd found so far who didn't like Jeri, but had she disliked her enough to kill her?

Cady's whereabouts were still unaccounted for at the time of Jeri's murder, but so what?

I'd gotten a weird vibe from Molly at the attorney's office yesterday, like she knew more than she was telling. Was it anything important to the case? And what about her comment that Jeri thought Cady Faye Catering might go out of business? What was that all about? Did it have anything to do with Jeri's death? I didn't see how.

If I was going to figure out who killed Jeri I needed to stretch my thinking, I decided. The only thing left to do was play a hunch, imagine the worst in somebody who seemed totally innocent, and connect the dots in a way I hadn't considered before.

I swung into the shopping center half expecting to see Jack Bishop and his black Land Rover there—or maybe that was just wishful thinking. I parked outside the front entrance to Cady Faye Catering, gulped down the last of my mocha frappuccino, grabbed my things, and went inside.

Faye was talking with a mother and daughter—they had a definite we're-planning-a-wedding look about them—so I went into her office to wait. I intended to go over the menu with her and make double-sure everything was set for tonight.

I was too keyed up to sit, so I paced back and forth. Honestly, I didn't know how Faye could work in the tiny office. The furniture was jammed together and packed with all kinds of stuff—including, I realized, the green duffel bag I'd seen in here earlier, which was still on the floor by the file cabinet.

Okay, that was weird.

I'd thought the duffel belonged to Faye but maybe it didn't because she hadn't taken it home. So it could have belonged to somebody who worked for her—someone who'd planned a getaway complete with sexy lingerie.

But whoever it was apparently didn't want to claim the duffel from the boss' office, probably because the owner assumed Faye had gone through the bag looking for an I.D. tag, as Wendy and I had done when we'd found it in the employee lounge. That would alert Faye to an illicit affair or perhaps a kinky lingerie fetish—something few people wanted to share with their employer.

Then it hit me that the duffel must have belonged to Jeri. She'd probably planned a few days with her married boyfriend after her shift ended here at Cady Faye, but had been killed. After all, she was having an affair. The dating phase of a relationship called for sexy lingerie and hot getaways.

Of course, maybe Jeri wasn't the only person here who was having an affair. The duffel could belong to most anyone at the catering company or the girls from Maisie's Costume Shop who'd been in the employee lounge the day Jeri died.

"No need to worry about us," Faye said, as she breezed into the office. She sat at her desk and plucked a file folder from one of the stacks. "Everything is under control."

Faye didn't seem concerned or offended that I'd come to check on things, which was a real relief. While I enjoy an occasional confrontation, I didn't want to get into anything with her, especially on a day as important as this one.

"It's all set?" I asked, sitting down in front of her desk.

She opened the file. "Maisie's will be here with the costumes this afternoon. The servers and bartenders are scheduled and will arrive shortly. The food is being prepared in our kitchen right now, exactly as the clients requested. Those detectives gave us access to the ice room so the ice sculptures will be on display. Everything— absolutely everything—we're responsible for will come off flawlessly at the Brannock party tonight, just as I promised."

She didn't come off smug or snarky about it, just confident and anxious to let me know she had everything under control.

"Great," I said, and heaved a little sigh of relief. "And Cady is okay? She'll be at the event to oversee the food?"

Faye's high-wattage smile dimmed for a second or two, then beamed once more.

"Cady is fine," she assured me, with a calmness that made me think she'd said those same words a zillion times before. "Please believe me, Haley. I have everything under control at my company. Everything."

Though I'd had my doubts, I could see that Faye did indeed have all phases of the business firmly in hand. No wonder it had grown three times over in the past year.

"And to ensure you're completely happy with everything," Faye said, "I will be at the Brannock party tonight overseeing things."

"Thank you, Faye," I said, rising from my chair.

"See you tonight," she said.

I gave her a little wave and left the building.

I walked across the parking lot toward my Honda feeling as if a huge weight had lifted. Just as Faye had always told me, everything would be great for the Brannocks' party tonight.

And things would look pretty darn good for me, too, I

realized.

I pictured next week's office meeting at L.A. Affairs. Everyone would be there. Priscilla would walk to the podium and announce that I'd discovered a fabulous new catering company. Everyone would be in awe. Priscilla would ask me to stand. I'd rise and channel my mother's gracious smile and a pageant queen wave. Everything would be perfect. Unless—

I stopped in my tracks at the front fender of my car.

What if there really was another murder tonight? Suppose whoever had killed Jeri showed up and targeted another victim?

Oh, crap.

A new, horrifying scenario played out my head that might take place at L.A. Affairs' next weekly office meeting: Priscilla announcing that the company's reputation had been flushed and it was all my fault— followed by everyone watching as I was escorted out of the building by a security guard.

I couldn't let that happen.

I unlocked my Honda and dropped into the driver's seat. I'd looked at this case from several different sides but hadn't come up with anything—except that there was a huge chunk of info missing. If only I could figure out what it was.

Then it hit me.

Yes, something big and important was missing from the investigation, but something equally big and important was holding it together. There was a common thread that connected everything—divorce and cheating spouses. Jeri and her married boyfriend; Jack's divorce case that had brought him to the Cady Faye Catering shopping center; Jeri's roommate who worked for a divorce attorney; the duffel bag packed for an illicit getaway.

I knew of only two places to find info on divorce and cheating spouses—Jack Bishop and Molly at the attorney's office.

I pulled out my cell phone and called Jack. He didn't answer so I left him a message asking for info on his cheating husband case.

"I'm going to the office of that divorce attorney who's plastered his picture all over the place, Rowland Horowitz," I said. "It's in Burbank. Call me. I'll meet you somewhere."

I started my car and headed out.

* * *

I was passing Studio City on the 101 freeway when my cell phone rang. I switched on my Bluetooth thinking it was Jack calling back, but it was Marcie.

"Great news," she said. "Are you sitting down?"

"Yes," I said, because, technically, I was.

"Our Flirtatious bags came in!" Marcie exclaimed.

I nearly veered onto the shoulder.

"Oh my God! Your friend came through for us at Nordstrom?" I asked.

"She just called me," Marcie said. "But here's the thing."

I hate it when there's a thing.

"We have to pick them up right away," Marcie said. "She can't hold them long. Everybody wants one of these bags and there could be a throw-down right there in the handbag department if anybody realizes she's holding them back."

I mentally ran through my schedule for the day. I had

to talk to Molly at the lawyer's office, find out what was up with Jack's divorce case, check on a few last minute details for the Brannock party, arrive at their house early enough to oversee the party prep—and, hopefully, solve Jeri's murder or at least find a viable suspect.

Picking up two fabulous handbags from Nordstrom would be no problem.

"I got this," I told her.

"Awesome," Marcie said.

"I'll call you when I have them," I promised and we hung up.

I exited the freeway and drove to the office of attorney Rowland Horowitz on Alameda Avenue, parked in the lot behind the building and went inside. Two women were seated on opposite sides of the waiting room filling out forms. A woman I didn't recognize was working at the desk behind the receptionist's window. None of them looked happy to be there.

I approached the window and asked, "Is Molly here?"

A few seconds passed before she lifted her head to look at me. She was mid-forties and had a definite I-hate-everyone-especially-young-pretty-women look about her.

"She's out."

"Do you know when she'll be back?" I asked.

"No," she replied. "What do you need?"

I didn't want to cause Molly any problems by admitting I was here for something personal, so I said, "I'll come back later."

I left the office mentally re-shuffling my plan for the day, then everything flew out of my head when I spotted Jack Bishop standing beside my car. I'd wanted to talk to him but I hadn't expected him to meet me here. Still, it's always a treat to see a hot-looking guy so early in the day.

Jack, however, didn't seem so pleased to see me despite my fabulous brown business suit and my even more fabulous Louis Vuitton handbag. I decided to come right to the point.

"I'm thinking there's a connection between your divorce case and the murder at Cady Faye Catering," I said.

"The murder you're not supposed to be involved with?" Jack asked.

"That's the one."

Really, I didn't know why Jack wasted his breath cautioning me not to get involved with this sort of thing. He knew what I was like.

"So what happened?" I asked.

Jack gave me semi stink eye for a few seconds, just to show he wasn't pleased with what I was doing, which I took as a semi compliment.

"I started tailing the guy as he left his apartment complex in Encino," Jack said. "He drove to the shopping center, stopped near the construction site. A woman got out and he drove away."

"Who was the woman?" I asked.

"Not my concern," Jack said. "I followed him down Ventura Boulevard to the McDonald's. He went inside, but came out again a few minutes later. The guy drove to his place, swapped cars, and went back to the shopping center. A block away, the same woman was on foot. He picked her up."

I got a weird feeling.

"Pictures?" Jack asked.

My weird feeling got weirder.

"Sure," I said, but I was pretty sure I already knew who'd I'd see in the photos.

Jack pulled his cell phone from his pocket, tapped the keys, then handed it to me. On the screen was the image of a white Mercedes parked in the shopping center. A man I didn't recognize was behind the wheel. The woman getting out was Cady.

Oh, crap.

Chapter 10

I'd seen a photo of Cady's husband in Faye's office so I knew this guy wasn't him. I told Jack who she was as I paged through the series of surveillance pictures he'd taken that day. When I came across a photo of Cady and the guy kissing, I knew she was having an affair. Jack didn't seem surprised.

"The thing with her arriving, then leaving, and him picking her up on the street and driving back again in a different vehicle is suspicious," I said.

It explained, though, why some of the employees at the catering company reported seeing Cady there earlier, and why they'd thought they'd seen her car was in the parking lot.

"It could have been something innocent," Jack said. "They're in love. Maybe she wanted to see him again. Maybe they had a fight and one of them wanted to apologize."

"Cady is really high-strung," I said. "I can totally see her walking into the kitchen and getting overwhelmed with the day's work. Three events in one day. That's a lot. Maybe she couldn't face it without another hug from her boyfriend."

"Maybe she forgot something," Jack said. "She called him and he brought it to her."

Those were all believable, reasonable scenarios. Still, something didn't seem right.

"So why swap cars?" I asked. "Maybe the guy thought he was being followed."

Jack looked mildly irked at my suggestion that he'd been discovered, but he didn't say so.

"Or maybe Cady killed Jeri," Jack said.

I'd considered that possibility before, but still couldn't connect all the dots.

"There's no motive—at least, not one I've found," I said. "And Cady was a wreck when Lourdes told her Jeri was dead. An absolute wreck. She lost it, big-time."

Jack and I both stood there for a while looking at the photos on his phone.

"The whole thing is suspicious," I said.

"It is," Jack agreed. "I talked to the cops."

Okay, this surprised me, but I guess it shouldn't have. Jack wasn't some rogue private detective operating on the fringes of the law, dodging cops and formal investigations.

"The detectives assigned to the case?" I asked.

"Grayson," he said.

That explained why Dan had gone been back to question Cady, and why he'd come to Holt's and asked me about her arrival on the day of the murder. Obviously, he was investigating Cady. But since he'd made no arrest, it seemed he hadn't uncovered any conclusive evidence.

I handed Jack's phone back to him.

"Let me know if anything shakes loose," he said.

"I will," I said, and was pleased he hadn't told me not to get further involved with the investigation.

Jack got in his Land Rover and drove away. I stood in the parking lot thinking about everything I'd just learned about Cady.

True, her behavior was odd, weird, and more than a little suspicious. But having an affair, arriving at Cady

Faye Catering only to leave on foot and then return in a different vehicle was a long way from committing a murder.

I dug my keys out of my purse as a car pulled into the lot and swung into a space near the rear entrance to the law firm. Molly got out juggling her purse, a bundle of mail, and a tray of coffees from Starbucks.

I walked over. She didn't look so happy to see me.

"I have to get inside," Molly said, and hurried toward the building's rear entrance.

I didn't see any reason to finesse this conversation, so I asked, "Why did Jeri think Cady Faye Catering would go out of business?"

"She just did, that's all," Molly said.

Then something hit me.

I stepped in front of her, forcing her to stop and said, "Horowitz is handling Cady's divorce, isn't he?"

"We're not supposed to talk about those things," Molly said, and ducked around me.

"Jeri was your roommate. You mentioned it to her, right?" I got in front of her and put my hand on the door as if I was going to open it for her, but didn't. "Right?"

"Yes, okay, fine," Molly told me. "I mentioned it to her. We're handling Jeri's boyfriend's divorce. I knew Jeri and Cady worked at the same place. I thought Jeri had told her to come here."

"But Jeri hadn't referred her?" I asked.

"No," Molly said. "And she was really upset when I told her what was going on."

"It had something to do with the terms of Cady's divorce?" I asked.

"Don't you think I feel bad enough about this?" Molly demanded. "I shouldn't have said anything to Jeri

---

about what was going on. Now she's dead."

Molly pushed past me and disappeared into the building.

I headed back to my car, my mind whirling.

Cady's divorce had riled Jeri big-time and had caused her to predict the catering company would go out of business. But had that somehow evolved into a murder?

Maybe.

I got into my car and Detective Dan Grayson popped into my head. I considered telling him what I'd just learned from Molly, the possible motive I'd uncovered. But I didn't know if he already knew about it.

No way did I want to look like an idiot by announcing my fantastic break in the case if it was old news to him. Yet, if he didn't already know about it, I really didn't want him to find his way to the law firm, question Molly, and learn that I'd already been there getting info that I hadn't told him about.

I dug through my purse, found the business card he'd given me, and called him. His voicemail picked up so I left a message.

* * *

The Brannocks' home was in an older neighborhood off Fairfax Avenue, on a street with small, well-maintained houses in the million-plus dollar range. Parking was always at a premium and today was no exception. As I drove past the house I saw that the street parking was all taken, and the Brannocks' driveway was jammed with a florist's delivery van and trucks from the construction crew. A Cady Faye Catering van was just pulling up; I was relieved to see they were here on time.

I'd already been here once today, this afternoon when I'd come by to make sure everything was on schedule. The Brannocks wanted an outdoor party so I'd worked with Webber's Florist and Lyle, the guy who owned the construction company that L.A. Affairs often used for this sort of event, to transform their backyard.

Green, orange, and white—the colors of the Irish flag—had been used in all the floral arrangements. Lyle and his crew had strung twinkle lights, wired the sound system for the band that would arrive later, and set up buffet tables, bars, and seating groups with comfy furniture. The swimming pool would be dyed green, filled with goldfish—I'd been assured the green water wouldn't do them any harm—then covered with plexiglass and used as a dance floor.

It wouldn't be a St. Patrick's Day bash without lots of alcohol. The mixology

crew I'd hired was keeping it green with emerald mint martinis, kiwi coladas, honeydew mimosas, and, of course, green beer.

Cady Faye Catering had planned a menu of Irish stew, corn chowder, corned beef brisket and cabbage, and an array of green finger foods. The dessert bar—where I intended to spent a great deal of my time this evening— would feature mint chocolate pudding, and cupcakes topped with sugar shamrocks.

On my earlier visit this afternoon, I'd seen that everything was going smoothly and was on schedule, so I'd seen no need to hang around—especially when I had pressing personal business to take care of.

I'd dashed over to Nordstrom at The Grove, just a few minutes away, to pick up the Flirtatious handbags Marcie's friend was holding for us. She was at lunch, so I had to wait around for about fifteen minutes. No big deal. I'd distracted myself looking at—okay, trying on—capris and sundresses. I mean, really, I had to have something appropriate to wear with my fabulous, yummy yellow Flirtatious satchel, right?

Somehow, time had gotten away from me. I'd picked up the Flirtatious handbags—concealed in a shopping bag to avoid a stampede if they were seen—and headed back to the Brannock home. The party wasn't schedule to start for another hour-plus, so I wasn't seriously late.

I drove past their house and turned at the corner, looking for a parking space on a nearby street. As events went, the Brannocks' was easier than most but I still had to focus on the job. That meant I had to put the whole thing about Cady's divorce and Jeri's murder out of my head.

I still hadn't heard back from Dan. I guess my maybe-I-found-something-important message wasn't all that important to him.

A spot at the curb was open so I swooped in, gathered my things, and headed back toward the Brannocks' street. The neighborhood was quiet. The sun was setting, casting shadows. Tall trees rustled slightly.

Up ahead just a little farther down the block, a gray Honda Pilot stopped in the street. It idled there for a few seconds, then Cady got out.

I froze.

Cady waved to the driver and blew a kiss. The Pilot drove off and she started walking toward the Brannock home.

Even though I knew Cady was having an affair and had been to an attorney, it made my blood boil seeing it played out in front of me. Of course, I knew nothing about Cady's marriage, her husband, or what kind of relationship they had—except for a couple of unfavorable comments I'd heard from Faye and Lourdes. I knew I shouldn't judge, but it bugged me just the same.

I followed Cady, my mind whirling with everything I knew about Jeri's murder and my suspicion that Cady was involved. I knew this wasn't the time to discuss it with her, not at tonight's event, anyway. I could do it tomorrow.

Or could I?

The green duffel bag sprang into my head.

Oh my God, was it hers? Did it belong to Cady?

It was packed with sexy clothes for a romantic getaway and she was having an affair, so it definitely could have belonged to her.

What if Cady was planning to leave town tonight after the event? What if she was gone a long time and days passed before I got the chance to talk to her?

I quickened my pace. Cady didn't seem to realize I was behind her. I followed her around the corner and down the Brannocks' street, and caught up with her just as she got to the Cady Faye Catering van parked in the driveway.

The rear doors were open. Nobody else was around. I saw that the van was empty except for a couple of bins of cutlery, some aluminum foil and plastic wrap. I figured everyone had already ferried the food to the buffet tables out back and were busy setting up.

"Hi, Cady," I said.

She gasped and spun around.

"Oh, Haley, it's you." She plastered both hands against her chest.

"I saw you get out of that Honda Pilot," I said, and nodded down the block. "Your boyfriend's SUV."

Cady froze, then shook her head. "No. No, you're mistaken."

"Rowland Horowitz," I said. "He's your attorney."

"How did you know? Who told you?" Her eyes widened. "Oh, God. You didn't tell Faye, did you? Does Faye know?"

Okay, having her sister find out she was leaving her husband and getting a divorce seemed like an odd thing to be upset about right now, but I went with it.

"Faye wouldn't like it, would she?" I said.

Cady's clinched her fists and her cheeks turned red.

"I *hate* her," she hissed. "I absolutely *hate* her. This is her fault. All of it."

I didn't have a chance to ask what she meant because she kept going.

"All I wanted to do was make a few cupcakes for friends, for kids' birthdays. Just a hobby. Something I could have fun with," Cady said. "But no. That wasn't good enough. It wasn't big enough. Faye jumped in the middle of it—just like she jumps in the middle of everything I do. We had to start a catering company. Nothing would do but for her to take over."

"You didn't want it?" I asked.

"And we couldn't have just a simple, ordinary catering company," Cady told me. "It had to be the biggest, the best. It had to keep getting bigger and better."

Cady was becoming more and more agitated. I got the feeling she'd been holding this in for a long time.

"Faye pressured you to do more?" I asked.

"Faye and everybody else," Cady said. "My husband. He saw what the company was bringing in. He started in on me, too. Do more, work harder. All he cared about was that stupid catering company."

I remembered that Faye had mentioned Cady's husband was very interested in the catering business, which didn't seem to make Faye happy at all.

"Neither of them cares about me," Cady said. "They only care about how much work I do, and how much money they can make off of me."

"So you found a boyfriend," I said.

Cady closed her eyes for a few seconds and drew in a big breath. "Yes," she whispered.

"You two were planning a romantic trip," I said. "That's why you brought the green duffel bag with you to work."

"It was going to be perfect," she murmured, "spending time with someone who loves me for myself, not for what he can get out of me."

"That's why you wanted a divorce," I said.

"Yes, and I didn't care what it took," Cady said, growing angry again.

"Including killing Jeri?" I asked.

Cady froze. She looked at me as if she hadn't understood my question. "That wasn't my fault."

She turned around and started sorting through the bins in the back of the delivery van, and said, "That girl at the attorney's office shouldn't have told Jeri what was going on. It was supposed to be confidential."

Oh my God, was I right? Had Cady murdered Jeri?

I heard the cutlery clink as Cady dug through it, my mind spinning, fitting the pieces of Jeri's death together.

"Actually," Cady said, "anyone in my position would have done the same thing."

"Murder Jeri?"

Cady spun around holding a butcher knife in her hand.

Oh, crap.

Chapter 11

"I told you that wasn't my fault," Cady said, pointing the knife at me. "I had to give that miserable excuse for a husband my portion of the business. I had to. It's the only way he would agree to the divorce."

Wow. That was a really big knife. It took me a few seconds to drag my gaze from the blade back to Cady, then another few seconds to understand what she had just told me.

"You gave your portion of Cady Faye Catering to your husband?" I asked.

"If I hadn't, the whole thing would have dragged on for ages," Cady said. She shook her head. "I wanted out. Now."

A huge, missing chunk of Jeri's murder fell into place. Jeri would have known that with Cady gone and her husband—a man Faye couldn't stand—becoming involved, the company would likely fall apart.

"You didn't tell Faye what you were doing?" I asked.

Cady tapped the flat of the knife against her palm. "Of course not. I couldn't tell Faye. She'd have fought me on it—like she fights me on everything."

"When Jeri found out what you were doing, she confronted you," I said.

"Oh, yes," Cady said. "Jeri was so concerned about Faye. Faye was great. Faye was wonderful. Faye would be so hurt. Faye did so much for everyone else. Faye,

Faye, Faye!"

Cady made a slashing motion with the knife. I took a step back.

"The day Jeri confronted you," I said, hoping to distract her, "did you explain how you felt?"

"I had no choice," Cady said, waving the knife around. "Sometimes I slip into the building through the construction site next door so Faye won't see me and start in on everything."

A mental light bulb lit up in my head. No wonder some of the servers said they thought they'd seen Cady in the building that day—she'd actually been in there.

"I put my duffel bag in the employee lounge with the other bags to disguise it. Somebody would have noticed it in my office," Cady said. "And it was a good thing I did because here came Jeri, hunting for me. Sent by Faye to track me down."

I got a yucky feeling in my stomach as I realized that my presence at Cady Faye Catering that day had been one of the reasons Faye had asked Jeri to find Cady.

"Jeri found me, of course, and insisted we go into the ice room," Cady said. "She started in on me about how she knew the details of my divorce, how awful she thought it was, how I was abandoning the business and it would be all my fault if everyone lost their job. I couldn't take it!"

Cady hadn't always seemed completely stable to me. I could see why the confrontation with Jeri might have pushed her too far.

I only hoped the conversation we were having wouldn't push her too far again—especially with that butcher knife in her hand.

"And then—then—she insisted I tell Faye what I'd done," Cady said.

"No way were you doing that," I said.

"I tried to get away from her," Cady said, tearing up. "I tried. I really tried. I even climbed the stairs up to that water tank to get away. But she came after me. She just kept coming."

"So you hit her and pushed her into the water tank," I said.

"No." Cady shook her head frantically. "I—I didn't push her into the water. I hit her. Not hard. I just wanted her to leave me alone. My ring scratched her face. It was an accident. I swear. But she became enraged. She tried to push me down the steps, so I—I—hit her and ran away."

"You hit her hard," I said.

"I didn't mean to," Cady insisted.

"She hit her head on something—the wall, one of those railings, something," I said, "and she fell into the water and drowned."

"I didn't mean for that to happen!" Cady screamed and pounded her palms against her head, still clutching the knife.

Okay, Cady was seriously losing it. I tried to calm her down.

"It's all right," I said. "It was an accident. You didn't mean for any of it to happen. I can see that. So will everyone else."

Cady stopped screaming. Her gaze bored into me.

"You're going to tell Faye, aren't you?" she said.

Of course, I was going to tell Faye—I was going to tell anyone who would listen—but this didn't seem like the best time for complete honestly.

"No!" Cady lunged at me and swung the knife. The blade sliced the sleeve of my jacket. I scrambled out of the way.

Cady screamed again, threw down the knife, and took off running. I tossed my handbag and portfolio into the van and followed her. She dodged between the vehicles parked in the driveway. I was close behind as we ran through the gate into the Brannocks' backyard.

Servers in leprechaun costumes, the caterers, the bartenders were all busy setting up. Construction workers were stringing lights, and three guys from the florist were arranging flowers on the buffet tables. The band was tuning up. Nobody seemed to notice as Cady ran past with me close behind.

"Stop!" I shouted as Cady circled the pool. "Stop!"

I was winded, and running in three-inch pumps wasn't easy.

Cady stopped. She was breathing hard. Maybe she was out of breath, too, or she felt safe with the pool separating us.

"Look, Cady, this whole thing is understandable," I said, which wasn't true, of course, but I needed to catch my breath. "You can explain everything."

"No!" Cady screamed.

Two electricians stringing lights on the shrubbery turned and looked at us.

"Call the police," I said to them.

"No!" Cady screamed again.

"Now," I said to the guys. "Call 9-1-1. Hurry!"

"No!"

Cady's scream revved up louder and louder. I turned. She was a couple of feet away, running toward me. She hit me with a full body blow. Back I went, Cady on me, and we fell into the pool.

The water closed over me. I tried to get away, but Cady held on. We sank deeper and deeper into the pool. I struggled, trying to get free. My lungs hurt. I tried to hit her, knock her off of me, but the water softened the blows.

Panic set it. Frantic, I fought, pushing her away. Nothing helped. She kept grabbing me, pulling me deeper into the water.

Something looped my waist and yanked me backward. Stunned, I exhaled as I was dragged upward. My head broke the surface and I gulped in a huge breath of air.

Oh my God, what had happened?

I spun around and saw Dan's head bobbing in the water next to me. He caught my arm and pulled me to the side of the pool. I grabbed the edge.

"Stay here," he said.

Dan dived under again. One of the electricians went in after him. A few seconds later they came to the surface holding Cady between them. As soon as her head cleared the water, she started screaming.

* * *

The Brannocks' St. Patrick's Day party was a rip-roaring success—or so it seemed as I looked out onto the backyard through their kitchen window. The police had already left, thankfully before the party guests showed up, after taking statements from everyone, gathering evidence, and taking Cady away. Nadine and Xander Brannock had given Dan and me dry clothes to change into; the electrician had gone home with everyone's thanks.

"More coffee?"

I was seated at their kitchen table, grateful that the Brannocks' housekeeper had made a pot just for me.

My hair was still wet, my makeup was ruined, and I

had on Nadine's yoga pants and a sweatshirt. Not a look I'd have gone for under other circumstances, but I was okay with it for now.

"Sure," I said, and held out my cup.

She filled it and moved away as voices drifted in from the direction of their dining room. Nadine and Xander walked into the kitchen. Dan was with them. He had on what I guessed were sweats that belonged to Xander.

Detective Elliston, whom I'd seen here early but who hadn't bothered to jump into the pool to save me, had left.

"Feeling better?" Xander asked.

"I'm good," I said.

Neither Nadine nor Xander seemed troubled that a murderer had been at their house, that their pool was nearly the scene of another crime, or that the police had been there. They both worked in Hollywood. It was just another party to them.

"Let me know if you need anything, Haley," Nadine said. She nodded toward the backyard. "We'd better get back out there. Xander?"

He followed her out the door.

Dan joined me at the table. The housekeeper brought him a cup of coffee, then disappeared.

"I guess I owe you for pulling me out of the pool," I said.

Dan grinned. "All part of the service, ma'am."

"How did you get here?" I asked.

I remembered yelling at one of the electricians to call the police just before Cady knocked me into the pool, but I couldn't understand how Dan could have gotten to the Brannocks' so quickly.

"I wish I could say I donned my superhero cape and

flew," Dan said, "but Elliston and I were already here questioning Faye Delaney."

I guess I hadn't seen their plain vanilla detective car because, like me, they'd had to park on a different street and walk over.

"You figured out what was up with Cady and her divorce?" I asked. "I was way ahead of you, wasn't I?"

"The receptionist in Horowitz's office was anxious to tell us everything," he said. "By the time we got to the catering company, everybody was gone. One of the girls there told us where Faye and Cady had gone."

"Did Faye know any of this?" I asked.

Dan shook his head. "Claimed she didn't."

I felt kind of sorry for Faye. She'd learned about her family problems in the worst way, and not only had she lost her business but her sister as well.

I couldn't help wondering which troubled her the most.

I wondered, too, about the duffel bag she'd kept in her office. Had she known it belonged to Cady? Did she have any idea what Cady was up to? Did she suspect she'd killed Jeri?

Good questions, but ones I figured I could only speculate about.

There was no need speculating about whether Faye would open another catering business, however. I knew she would—hopefully, without any family involvement.

Dan and I sat at the table for a few more minutes and just as I thought we were about to have yet another middle-school moment, he rose from his chair.

"I'd better go," he said. "Lots of paperwork to take care of."

I nodded and got up. We walked outside. Twinkle

lights illuminated the darkness. Music flowed from the backyard, joined by raised voices and laughter. I'd put together a heck of a party, all right.

"Thanks again for saving my life," I said.

Dan just stood there for a few seconds, then said. "I wish things had turned out differently."

"You mean you wish you hadn't saved me?" I asked.

"I wish I weren't leaving," he said. "My sister lives in Fresno. Her husband died last year in a car accident. She's having trouble with her teenage boys. I'm taking a leave of absence for a while to help out."

"Oh."

I hadn't expected that I wouldn't see him again soon—or that I'd feel so disappointed about it.

He gave me a little wave and left.

"Haley? Haley?" someone called.

Nadine hurried toward me. Beside her was a tiny gray haired woman sporting a green track suit, light-up leprechaun earrings, and a sparkling shamrock broach.

"This is my mom Lorelei," Nadine said. "She's very impressed with the event you put together for us."

"Well, everything is marvelous, just marvelous," Lorelei said. "I'd love for you to handle my next event. It's quite large, and it's coming up soon. Can you do that?"

I'd definitely need to redeem myself at L.A. Affairs after word got out what had happened at the Brannock event.

"I'll have to clear it with my office manager," I said.

"Haley works for L.A. Affairs," Nadine explained.

"Well, of course, I should have known. Your company does wonderful work. I've used them before, many times," Lorelei said. "In fact, I'm going to call

Priscilla first thing in the morning. I'm going to insist that you handle our luncheon, Haley."

I got a weird feeling.

"A luncheon?" I asked.

"Yes, our organization has an annual luncheon."

My weird feeling got weirder.

"Perhaps you've heard of us?" Lorelei said. "We're the Daughters of the Southland."

Oh, crap.

THE END

Dear Reader,

There's more Haley out there! If you enjoyed this novella, check out the other books in the series. They're available in hardcover, paperback, and ebook editions.

Looking for even more mystery? Meet Dana Mackenzie, my newest amateur sleuth, in Fatal Debt and Fatal Luck. Both are available in paperback and ebook editions.

I also write historical romance novels under the pen name Judith Stacy. Check them out at www.JudithStacy.com.

More information is available at www.DorothyHowellNovels.com., where there's always a giveaway going on! Join my Dorothy Howell Novels Facebook page, sign up for my newsletter, and follow me on twitter @DHowellNovels.

Thanks for adding my books to your library and recommending me to your friends and family.

Happy reading!
Dorothy

P.S. Keep reading for a peek at Fatal Debt, the launch book in the Dana Mackenzie mystery series.

Fatal Debt

A Dana Mackenzie Mystery

by Dorothy Howell

Dana Mackenzie finds work at a faceless financial institution—it's either this or piercing ears at the mall—but she has no intention of following the corporate offices' heartless orders.

She's sent to the home of an elderly couple with instruction to repossess their television, but instead finds sweet old Mr. Sullivan murdered. Investigating the case is homicide detective Nick Travis, Dana's high school crush, who's still harboring a dark secret from their past.

Dana agrees to help Mr. Sullivan's grieving family locate his grandson, a guy with a surprising new lifestyle. Her good intentions put her in the thick of the murder investigation and on a collision course with the killer.

FATAL DEBT
by Dorothy Howell

Chapter One

"Repo the Sullivans's TV," Manny said, gesturing to the print-out on his desk.

"What? The Sullivans? No way," I told him.

"Today," he said. "They're too far past due. We can't carry them."

"Come on, Manny, not the Sullivans," I said. "They're nice people. They've had an account with us for twenty years, or something. I can't repossess their television."

Manny Franco who, technically, was my supervisor—though I disagreed with the disparity in our positions on many levels—lowered himself into his chair and dug his heels into the carpet to roll himself up to his desk.

"We never should have made that loan. They can't afford it," he said, swiping his damp forehead with his palm.

Manny was always stressed. He was only an inch taller than me—and at five-feet, nine-inches I'm tall for a girl—and outweighed me by at least a hundred pounds. He wore his black hair long and slicked back in waves. His suits always looked a little rumpled and his collar a size too small.

I was sitting in the chair beside Manny's desk in the office of Mid-America Financial Services, a nationwide consumer finance company that granted personal loans, second mortgages, and did some dealer financing for things like TVs, stereos, and furniture.

I'd worked all sorts of jobs in the past few years. Data entry, waitressing, sales clerk, then a good job as an admin assistant for a major corporation that went under, taking me with it. Piercing ears at the mall landed me the job at Mid-America.

Something about snapping on latex gloves and driving a metal spike through the flesh of infants and children had impressed Mr. Burrows, the branch manager, and he'd hired me several months ago as an asset manager.

While that might sound like a fabulous job—that came with a fabulous salary—not so. But the big three-oh was on the horizon, I'd been unemployed *forever*, and I was still working on my B.A., so I didn't have a lot of options. Like many other people in the country, I'd been desperate for a paycheck. Besides, I hadn't decided what my future held—beyond taking over the world, the only thing I knew for sure I wanted to do with my life.

I liked justice. I liked the scales to balance, which was one of the things that appealed to me about my job with Mid-America. It gave me a chance to be judge, jury, and executioner, at times, to mete out a little justice for my customer's benefit and, sometimes, for Mid-America's benefit.

I didn't like it when things didn't even out.

According to Mid-America, the position of asset manager required that I telephoned customers who were behind on their payments and work with them to get their accounts up to date. I was okay with helping people get back on their feet, financially—I remember well the Summer of Spam, as I thought of it, when I was ten years old and my dad lost his job.

I was also expected to take whatever steps were necessary to collect Mid-America's accounts, including pursuing legal action and repossessing collateral. No way was I doing that, so I put my own twist on the position.

"The Sullivans are doing okay," I said to Manny, even though I knew they weren't. But I liked them, two sweet old people, both in their sixties.

"Repo the TV, Dana," Manny said.

"Mr. Sullivan lost his part-time job," I said.

Manny was unmoved. He'd heard this story a zillion times.

"He has another job lined up," I said, even though I knew it wasn't true. "They'll have the money soon."

Manny's gaze narrowed, studying me, like he thought maybe I was just shining him on—which I was. But I'm as good at the stare-down as anybody so I gazed right back at Manny without blinking an eye.

"I have to answer to Corporate on this," he said.

Corporate. What a bunch of jackasses.

"Pick up the TV, Dana. Now," Manny said, then turned to his computer. I gathered my stuff and left the office with one thought burning in my mind: how the heck was I going to get out of repoing the Sullivans' television and still keep my job?

* * *

I fumed as I drove out of Mid-America's parking lot and headed for the freeway. Luckily, I had on a favorite pants and jacket outfit, the sun shone bright, and I was treated to a gorgeous late October day here in Santa Flores.

The city was, admittedly, not one of Southern California's finest, even though it was situated half-way between Los Angeles and Palm Springs, at the base of the mountains leading up to the Big Bear and Lake Arrowhead ski resorts. But don't let that prestigious location give you any ideas. A few years back Santa Flores was dubbed the Murder Capital of America.

Yes, the Murder Capital of America was my home. A place where you could get killed for your shoes. I'd lived there all my life. My whole family lived there too, except my older brother who'd married and moved up north about a year ago; Mom's still giving him "another month or so" before she's sure he'll move back.

Like a lot of other places, things had gone badly for Santa Flores in the last few decades. The steel mill shut down, the railroad yard moved, the Air Force base closed. Gangs moved in from L.A. The real estate bubble burst. Businesses closed. The only thing on the upswing was the number of people out of work.

* * *

I took the 215 freeway north and exited on State Street—the Sullivans had been behind on their account so many times I knew the way to their house without my GPS—then made my way to Devon, a nice area—once—but that was before I was born. Gangs had brought drugs and violence. Some of the houses were abandoned, long ago falling to ruin. A few families valiantly kept up their yards and painted over the graffiti on their fences; most just hung on.

As I parked outside the chain link fence that

surrounded the Sullivans' little stucco home, I noted the place needed painting. The grass was dead. Old lawn chairs and broken flower pots were overturned beside the porch.

Despite everything, Arthur and Gladys Sullivan were sweet, loveable old people, the kind you couldn't say no to—though Mid-America should have said "no" to their last loan request. They were on a fixed income; their budget was tight. They'd needed five hundred dollars to fix their car, and Mr. Sullivan needed that car to get to his part-time job. Mid-America had approved the loan, picking up their 42-inch Sony television for collateral.

They'd fallen behind on their payments a few months ago but I'd let it go—thus, the *twist* I'd put on my job description—giving them time to get some money together. Now Manny—and Corporate—thought I'd held off too long. I had, but that didn't mean I was going to take their TV.

I got out of my Honda. The front gate squeaked when I opened it, the boards of the porch groaned, the screen door rattled. I knocked, hoping the Sullivans wouldn't be there. They were.

Mr. Sullivan opened the door also squeaking, groaning, and rattling. His file indicated he was 67. He looked older. His hair appeared more white than gray against his black skin. He wore denim jeans and a red flannel shirt buttoned at the collar; he walked on the backs of his corduroy house slippers.

He squinted at me and smiled, showing a missing bottom tooth, then turned back inside.

"Look who's here," he called. "It's that Mid-America girl."

I'm here to repo his TV and he's glad to see me.

Great.

"Dana Mackenzie," I said, reminding him of my name.

He led the way into the living room. The house was neat and clean, decorated with lace doilies and pictures of Jesus. It smelled like boiling beans and linoleum.

Mrs. Sullivan sat on a worn sofa wearing a floral house coat with snaps up the front. She was watching television, of course.

"Hi, Mrs. Sullivan," I said.

She glanced up at me. "Hi, honey."

"Mama's watching her stories," Mr. Sullivan said.

A soap opera, I realized, glancing at the screen.

Mr. Sullivan eased onto his threadbare recliner and I sat in a straight-backed chair beside him. We exchanged pleasantries and I stalled, but finally came to the point.

"I'm sorry, Mr. Sullivan, but my boss reviewed your account, and he wants me to pick up your television," I said.

He just looked at me, taking it in, making me feel worse, then shook his head.

"Well, if you got to, you got to." He looked over at his wife. "But how's Mama gonna watch her stories? She loves her stories. What's she gonna do?"

He wasn't so much asking me as musing aloud how he'd let her down.

If ever I'd been tempted to give a customer some money, this was it. They were old people. They didn't have much. The home they'd bought when they were young was decaying. The neighborhood they'd invested their time and emotion in had fallen to criminals. Their health was about gone. Not much was left for them— except Mrs. Sullivan's stories, and Mr. Sullivan's ability to let her watch them.

I'd be fired on the spot if I made a payment on a customer's account. A partial payment, a few cents, it wouldn't matter. Even if I loaned it to them, I'd be gone. And I couldn't afford to lose my job.

"We don't get money again until the first of the month," Mr. Sullivan said. "I've got Mama's medicine money. I could give you that."

I cringed.

"I'll call Leonard," I said.

Leonard was their grandson. He'd had an account with Mid-America some time back. Lots of families had accounts with us. It wasn't unusual. They passed us around and talked about us over holiday meals.

Leonard was about my age. He had trouble holding a job—not finding a job, like most people, just holding onto it. He'd been late on his payments more times than not, yet there was something very likeable about him. I had no problem calling him and asking for money on his grandparents' behalf.

"He's a good boy," Mr. Sullivan said. "We raised him, me and Mama, after his daddy died and his mama took off. He's got a new job. I'll call him. He'll help us out."

I felt more relieved than Mr. Sullivan appeared.

"I'll tell him to come by the house after he gets off work," Mr. Sullivan said. "Maybe he can drive me down to your office."

I didn't want to take the chance that something might come up, so I said, "I'll come back out and pick up the money."

"You come on back at supper time," Mr. Sullivan said.

I waved to Mrs. Sullivan, who didn't seem to notice, thanked Mr. Sullivan, and left.

* * *

In the short time I'd worked for Mid-America, the company had been bought out by a major conglomerate, then a mega-conglomerate, neither of which had done much except cause everyone a lot of unnecessary headaches.

Our office was located in downtown Santa Flores in a two-story building on Fifth Street. Just down the block were the post office, the courthouse, and all sorts of restaurants, bars, and office buildings.

Mid-America had one of the offices on the ground floor that offered great "signage," according to a guy in a thousand-dollar-suit who'd come out from the corporate office in Chicago to evaluate our location and formulate an enhanced marketing plan, and then had, apparently, forgotten we existed.

All I cared about was keeping our current location so I could look out our big plate glass window all day.

When I got back to the office Manny was more concerned with a possible foreclosure on a house out in Webster, a town about twenty minutes east of Santa Flores. He accepted my explanation of why I wasn't carrying a 42-inch Sony television with only a brief nod, and I got on with my work.

My desk sat at the rear of the office near Manny's. This placement was Corporate's decision, not mine. According to Mid-America's seating chart, the cashier who took payments from our walk-in customers sat at the counter up front. Just behind her were the two financial reps who handled the lending end of the business, along with Inez Marshall, their supervisor who was, thankfully, not in the office today. The beige furniture, walls, and carpet, and seascapes in plastic frames, were about as generic as an office could get.

The mail had been delivered while I was out, and I saw a neat stack of envelopes centered on my desk— Corporate had not bestowed upon us online bill-paying capability, despite our fabulous signage. I got to look at the mail before anyone in the branch because I was anxious to know which of my customers had paid. Getting money together to make a payment was tough for my customers. I didn't want to be calling them if their payment was at the cashier's desk waiting to be posted.

I'd just about reached the bottom of the stack when a familiar return address leaped off the envelope and smacked me between the eyes.

Nick Travis.

My breath caught and I felt a smile spread across my face. Oh, yeah, this was the boost I needed right now.

I'd known Nick Travis in high school. Everybody knew Nick Travis. Football team captain, student body president, gorgeous hottie. He'd dated my best friend, Katie Jo Miller, for a short while—a very short while— when Katie Jo and I were sophomores and Nick was in his senior year.

Nick got her pregnant, made her have an abortion, then dumped her and left town.

Imagine my surprise all these years later to find an account on Mid-America's books from Nick Travis. He'd financed a high-end television and sound system. I hadn't even known he'd moved back to Santa Flores.

When I'd seen Nick Travis's name on the computer

screen that day—and after I got myself up off the floor—I accessed his file and proceeded to learn everything there was to know about the man who'd ruined my best friend's life.

The copy of his driver's license that the TV dealer had provided indicated Nick was six-three, two hundred twenty pounds, brown hair, blue eyes. He'd moved back to Santa Flores a few months before the application was taken. He had checking and savings accounts at a credit union, two Visas with small balances, a Chevy that was financed, and a mortgage payment.

The mortgage surprised me because according to the application, Nick was unmarried. He had no dependents and paid no child support or alimony.

The shocker was that Nick worked for the Santa Flores Police Department as a detective. I guess they're pretty desperate these days—especially here in the Murder Capital of America.

Katie Jo's abortion had been rough. Her parents had been supportive but they were disappointed in their little girl. There were religious issues.

She stayed home for a long time. She wouldn't return phone calls. She refused to talk to anyone, even to me, her best friend. She was never the same after that. Neither were her parents. Neither was I.

The only one unscathed was Nick Travis.

I logged onto my computer and pulled up his account. A lot of people waited until the last minute to make their payment, getting it in to us just before it was considered late. Nick Travis was one of those people. According to his due date, today was the last day he could make his payment and avoid a late charge.

I looked at the computer screen, looked at his

payment, and thought about Katie Jo Miller.

I ripped Nick Travis's check into tiny pieces and dropped it into my trash can.

* * *

At 4:50 I pulled up Nick Travis's account on my computer and called his office.

"Travis," he barked, when he came on the line. He sounded as if he was just short of a bad mood. I was about to make his afternoon.

I identified myself with my sweetest voice.

"I'm calling because I was looking over your account and I noticed that today is the last day to avoid a late charge," I said, "and we haven't received your payment yet."

Silence. The cold, hard kind.

"I made that payment," he finally said.

I pictured cartoon-steam coming out of his ears.

"Well, it hasn't come in yet," I said. "You can bring it in, if you want to avoid the late charge."

"You close in five minutes."

I gasped—an Academy Award winning gasp—and said, "You're right. Looks like you'll have to pay that late charge."

I hung up feeling pleased with myself, and pleased for Katie Jo, too.

At five o'clock on the dot Carmen Chavez, our cashier, locked the door and began to count her cash drawer. Carmen was a few years younger than me, but was already married with a small child.

I was about to take off for the Sullivan place when a face appeared through the glass on our front door.

Nick Travis.

My heart did a little flip-flop.

I recognized him because he'd been into the office on previous months to make his payment. He'd changed so much I'd never have recognized him from high school.

Nick was taller now, bulkier as men got after their teenage years. In high school he'd been drop-dead gorgeous; now there was a blunted, more angular look to his face. Square jaw, strong chin, straight nose. Still good looking, but in a more rugged way.

He had on gray trousers, a navy blue sport coat, and a tie that actually looked good together. I wondered if he had a woman dressing him.

I was pretty sure Nick had recognized me from high school when he'd come into the office a few months ago and I'd waited on him at the counter. I'd seen that flash of recognition in his face, but he hadn't said anything.

Maybe he didn't like being reminded of high school—or Katie Jo Miller.

Or maybe he was just being a jerk.

I unlocked the door and peered at him, pretending I didn't know who he was.

"We're closed," I told him.

"You called me just now about my payment," he said.

I stared, still pretending.

"Nick Travis," he said.

"Oh, right. You're the one with the late payment," I said.

"I sent my payment," he told me. "In plenty of time."

"It was never received, obviously," I said. "You can make your payment, if you'd like. We'll post it tomorrow. You'll have that late charge by then."

He glared at me. "Fine."

I let him in and couldn't help but take a long look as he headed toward the counter. My heart did a little pitter-pat. To compensate, I stepped to the power position behind the counter.

"You might want to stop payment on that check you claim you sent," I said.

He pulled his checkbook from the pocket of his sport jacket and said, "That will cost me another twenty bucks on top of the late charge."

I gave him my too-bad-for-you shrug.

"This is the fourth time this has happened in the last five months," Nick said. He dashed off his check, then ripped it out of the book.

I made him stand there and hold it out for a few seconds before I took it.

My stomach felt a little queasy, but that was probably because I'd trashed his check this morning, though my I'm-feeling-guilty stomach roll was a little different from what I experienced at the moment.

Or maybe it was Nick. I always felt a little nervous when he came into the office, but that was because he was in law enforcement. Policemen always made me feel as if they knew everything I'd done wrong, like they could somehow see inside me and know about the lipstick I shoplifted from Wal-mart when I was fourteen.

"I need a receipt," Nick said.

Carmen was busy counting the day's payments so I wrote out a receipt. When I looked up again I caught him eyeing the office, using his police detective X-ray vision to check out my trash can, no doubt.

"Here," I said, distracting him with the receipt.

Nick tucked it inside his checkbook, then headed for the door. I followed. Once outside, he looked back and gave me a half grin.

Nick had a grin other men would have paid serious bucks for. The kind of grin that made women melt into their shoes. For a second, I got lost in that grin. I started to melt.

Katie Jo had reacted the same way. How many other women had, too?

I locked the door, shut down my computer and left the office.

* * *

The neighborhood seemed oddly quiet when I pulled up in front of the Sullivan house. No one was outside. No kids played in the yards. No music blared from the nearby houses, no dogs barked. The sun was going down, the light fading.

I got out of my car and climbed onto the porch. The front door stood open a few inches. I knocked and the door swung open a little more. A lamp burned in the living room and the television played softly; it sounded like a basketball game was on.

"Mr. Sullivan? Hello?" I called.

I figured I'd find him asleep in front of the TV so I stepped inside and leaned around the corner.

No one was there. I walked farther into the room. Movement off to my right, down the hallway, caught my attention a fraction of a second before a man barreled into me. He hit me on the right shoulder and knocked me backwards. I stumbled over something and sat down hard on my butt, my feet flying into the air, my head thumping on the side of the recliner. Stunned, I sat there for a second or two, then scrambled to my feet more mad than hurt.

"Hey!" I shouted. But I was talking to myself. The man was gone, the front door slammed shut.

I straightened my clothes, restoring some sort of personal dignity. A minute passed before it occurred to me that I still hadn't seen the Sullivans.

"Mr. Sullivan?" I called.

I crept down the hallway and peered into the first bedroom on the left.

Mr. Sullivan lay on the floor. Dead.

Dana and Nick's story continues
in the novella Fatal Luck.

Find out what happens when Nick finally confesses!

In the mood for some romance?

Here's a sneak peek at

Maggie and the Law

written under Dorothy's pen name, Judith Stacy.

What do a stage coach robbery, an ancient love goddess,
and the Rockies have in common?

They all lead to romance!

It's 1889 and university graduate Maggie Peyton has traveled alone to the wilds of Colorado to pull off the most daring deed humanity has ever witnessed. But when she meets Sheriff Spence Harding during a stage coach holdup, she realizes he could endanger her whole mission.

Spence must stick to the business of maintaining law and order in Marlow, Colorado. But newcomer Maggie is making it tough. He can't keep his eyes off of her—even though he suspects she's up to no good. This potential burglar just might steal his heart!

MAGGIE AND THE LAW

By Judith Stacy

Chapter One

Colorado, 1889

Men looked different when you were flat on your back.

At least, this one did.

Maggie Peyton gazed up at the man whose face hovered above hers. Dark, smoldering eyes bored into her. A corner of his lip turned back in a snarl. Hot breath puffed from his nose.

The hard floor pressed painfully against Maggie's back. His knees brushed her thighs. His long fingers pinned her shoulders down.

Bewildered, Maggie just stared at him.

For the last two hours he'd sat on the stagecoach seat across from her, rudely stretching out his legs to take up most of the room, but slouched down with his hat over his face seemingly sleeping—seemingly harmless. They were the only two passengers on board, and he'd barely spoken to her, except to introduce himself.

Then suddenly, a moment ago, this Mr. Spence Harding had bolted upright, grabbed her, dragged her onto the floor and jumped atop her. She'd been too stunned to think, to move. Now—

"Get off of me!" Maggie swung at him. Her palm slapped against his ear and jaw with a loud crack. His head whipped around. He loosened his grip.

Maggie scrambled away, kicking at his thighs. She rolled onto her side, trying to get to her feet.

He grabbed her, easily turning her onto her back again.

A scream tore from her throat. Blindly, she batted at him, slapping his face, his shoulder, his chest.

"Settle down!" His voice, deep and guttural, boomed as he grabbed both her hands. "The stage—"

"Let me go!"

"Be still!" He stretched her hands above her head and held them down.

Maggie's thoughts raced. No one else on board. No one to help her, except perhaps the driver up top. But could he even hear her screams above the thundering of the horses' hooves, the creak of the coach, the rush of the wind?

Panic overwhelmed her. Maggie kicked wildly, blindly, furiously.

"I told you, lady, just—yeow!" Spence grimaced, then anchored his leg over hers and slapped his hand across her mouth.

Maggie's heard pounded. She struggled, desperate to escape his grasp. He'd pinned her to the floor. She was helpless, totally at his mercy.

Bile rose in Maggie's throat. Her worst fear. When she'd made the decision to leave New York, take this trip west—totally alone—her personal safety had been a concern. But she'd never expected *this*.

Maggie gulped as she looked up at Spence Harding.

———

Beneath the brim of his black hat, his thick dark brows bunched together. His jaw tensed as his lips pressed into a thin, angry line.

The man was an animal. A beast. And he was huge. She'd noticed that the instant the two of them had boarded the stagecoach this afternoon in Keaton. Big shoulders and arms. Long legs. Meaty hands.

He'd ravish her. Murder her. Toss her body out of the moving coach. She'd never be heard from again. Her father would wait and worry, wonder what had become of his only child.

A little mewl gurgled in Maggie's throat as the man leaned down. She squeezed her eyes shut, her mind screaming in revulsion.

His leg shifted against hers. Maggie's eyes popped open. No, she couldn't—wouldn't—let this happen. She hadn't come this far, traveled for so long on such an important mission to have it end like this.

Maggie lurched, bared her teeth, and bit into his hand.

Spence jerked away. "Goddamn, son of a—"

Maggie wrestled from his grasp, groping for the seat, struggling to escape. Two big hands grasped her hips and sat her down hard on the floor. Spence glared at her, his eyes blazing.

"Stay down, before you get your fool head shot off," he commanded. "The stage is being robbed."

Maggie froze. Her gaze darted to the window, then back to him again. "The—what?"

"Outlaws are riding in." Spence drew his gun and rolled onto his knees, creeping toward the window. "The stage is being robbed. Stay on the floor."

She realized then that the stagecoach had picked up speed, bouncing and bucking worse than usual.

"Well, why didn't you simply say so?" Maggie demanded. Anger bubbled up inside her, chasing away the fear. "Did you think I wouldn't understand? That I couldn't grasp the concept? Did you—"

"For chrissake, lady, shut up!" He glanced back at her. "And get down on the floor!"

"Well!" Maggie glared right back at him. "Why don't *you* get on the floor?"

He raised from a crouch to peek out the window, then dipped his head and looked back at her.

"I've already been slapped, kicked and bit," Spence said. "I'll take my chances with the outlaws."

He turned back to the window and eased upward, his gun at the ready. Maggie rose to her knees, craning her neck to see around him.

Outside, men on horseback raced through the rugged terrain alongside the stagecoach. They would overtake the stage in moments.

Such a spectacle. Maggie stared, mesmerized by the churning of the horses' legs, the men's dusters snapping behind them, their hat brims bending in the wind, their drawn weapons.

She'd never witnessed such a sight. Not once, in all her travels with her father to the farthest corners of the world. Oh, if only he could be here to see this. How intrigued he would be.

A gunshot pierced the air. Spence retuned fire, then ducked, saw her peeking over his shoulder and pulled her to the floor.

"What the hell is wrong with you, lady? Stay down."

Another volley of gunfire sounded. Answering shots rang out, and Maggie guessed it came from the driver up top. A bullet tore through the door of the stagecoach, splintering the wood. Maggie grasped and flattened herself against the bucking floor. Spence pressed himself atop her.

"They're—they're really shooting at us," she whispered.

His face hovered inches above hers. Their gazes met and held in a long, lingering look. His features that had seemed so hostile, so forbidding only a short while ago, softened. The moment stretched endlessly. The two of them—strangers—caught in an age-old struggle for life itself.

"Are they going to kill us?" she asked.

His jaw tightened. "Not if I can help it."

He tried to rise but Maggie grasped his shirt with both hands and yanked him down gain. Visions of her life at her father's side flashed in her mind. Endless hours spent in lecture halls, dusty libraries and museums. Treks to tiny towns, remote villages, ancient ruins.

"I can't *die*," she wailed. "I haven't even *lived* yet."

Spence caught her wrists. "Look, lady—"

"I've never married," Maggie exclaimed. "Never produced a child, never even known a man!"

"I'd be happy to oblige you, honey, but all that takes a little more time than I've got right now." Spence pulled her hands free of his shirt and crept to the window.

Maggie pushed herself up, the meaning of his words dawning on her. Her cheeks flamed. "You think I wanted *you* to—to … right here in the stagecoach!"

Spence swore an oath, then fired his pistol out the window. Gunshots answered. He ducked, bobbed up and fired again, then dropped to the floor, his back braced against the seat.

"There're three of them coming in, covering both

sides of the stage," Spence said, his fingers quick and sure as he reloaded his pistol.

The stagecoach slowed. Maggie lifted her head. "Is it really a good idea to stop now?"

He spared her a quick glance. "You're not from around here, are you?"

"Well, no. Actually, I'm from—"

A gunshot boomed outside. Maggie gasped and ducked. The stagecoach stopped with a lurch. She lifted her gaze to see Spence pointing his pistol at one of the outlaws through the coach window. He didn't fire, though, as the other man pointed a rifle back at him. She looked out the window on the other side of the stage and saw two more outlaws pointing guns at them.

"Give me that gun and come on out of there," one of the outlaws said.

Spence glared at him for a few seconds, then glanced behind him and saw the others.

Maggie gulped. They were caught in a crossfire. Their situation was hopeless. He didn't stand a chance. Yet several tense seconds dragged by before Spence tossed his pistol out the window and got to his feet.

Bending low, he caught Maggie's arms and helped her up. Her limbs felt stiff, wooden. She wasn't sure she could stand on her own.

Spence leaned into her and spoke quietly. "Do whatever they say. Give them whatever they want." His brows drew together. "And keep your mouth shut."

Maggie followed him out of the stagecoach, her heart pounding and her knees trembling. He lifted her to the ground and stepped in front of her.

Good gracious, the man was tall. Maggie couldn't even see over his shoulder. He was wide and sturdy and strong, a formidable wall of protection in front of her.

She caught glimpses of the outlaws as they went about their work. Hard, weather-beaten faces. Dusty, unkempt clothing. If not thieves, they could have been farmers or miners. What had caused these seemingly ordinary men to turn to a life of crime? Maggie wondered.

While one of the men—the leader, she supposed—remained on his horse holding them at gunpoint, the other two climbed aboard the stagecoach.

"Driver's dead," one of them called out.

Maggie's stomach lurched. Dead? The man was dead? She gulped and said a quick prayer.

An oath so vile Maggie didn't know what some of the words meant rang out from the top of the coach. "There's no strongbox."

The man on horseback cursed, then shook his head. "We'll take the team," he said, then waved his rifle toward Maggie and Spence. "See what they got on them."

Both men jumped to the ground. The bigger of the two began unhitching the horses from the stagecoach, while the other approached Spence.

"Empty your wallet," he said.

Spence shifted his weight as he towered over the robber. Maggie sensed the tension in Spence, coiled like a snake ready to strike. His face in profile, she saw his tight jaw, his eyes as they flickered from the robber in front of him to the leader holding the rifle. For an instant, Maggie was sure she saw his mind working. Calculating. Looking for a way to get the upper hand.

Then finally, Spence pulled his wallet from his back pocket and handed over a handful of bills.

The outlaw turned to Maggie. He was young, she realized, seeing his smooth jaw and the few whiskers that had pushed through. Not much taller than herself, he was thin and bony in ill-fitting clothes, a shock of unruly hair sticking out from under his battered hat. She guessed him to be considerably younger than her own twenty-two years.

So young and already his life had taken this desperate turn. Maggie just looked at him. Oh, if only her father could be here to see this.

"What's your name?" she asked.

He squinted at her. "How's that?"

"Your name," Maggie repeated.

"It's Henry," he said, and shifted uncomfortably. "Now, you gotta give me your money, ma'am."

"How old are you?"

"Huh?"

"I said, how old are you/"

Spence turned and looked at her with bulging eyes. "Shut up," he hissed.

The boy glanced at the man on horseback, then back at Maggie again. "Look, ma'am, you've got to—"

"Fifteen? Sixteen?" Maggie asked. She looked him up and down. "Where is your mother?"

Spence glared at her as if she'd lost her mind.

"My mama's dead," Henry said, and stole a furtive glance at the gang leader once more. "Now, would you just give me your money—"

"Your mother is dead and *this* is what you've chosen to do with your life?" Maggie shook her head, trying to comprehend. She spread her arms. "What on earth made you do such a thing? Does it seem exciting? Did you do poorly at school? Have you no education? What was the turning point for you?"

The boy turned to Spence. "Is she not right in the head, or somet6hing?"

"Crazy as a loon." Spence caught her arm and leaned down. "Give the kid your money."

Maggie jerked away from him. "I am not crazy. How dare you say such a thing! I'm merely asking—"

A gunshot pierced the air. Maggie jumped. The gang leader nudged his horse and rode closer. "What the hell is going on over here?"

Henry gestured to Maggie. "Something's wrong with her."

The gang leader gave her a slow once-over. "She looks okay to me. Looks damn fine."

Maggie flushed at the man's bold gaze. Yet she couldn't let go of her concern for the boy.

"What possessed you to employ this boy in your … organization?" she asked. "Have you no regard for the young mind that is, at this very moment, being warped—perhaps permanently?"

"See?" Henry waved his hand at Maggie, as if she'd just confirmed his point.

All the men stared at her, bringing a new flush to Maggie's face and a wave of anger with it.

Her shoulders stiffened. "Now see here—"

"She's my wife's sister," Spence said. "I'm taking her to the asylum at Henderson."

"What?" she exclaimed. "How dare you suggest that I am somehow—"

He caught her arm again. "Calm down now, Sis. It's really for the best."

She jerked away from him. "What on earth are you talking about?"

"Shut up!" The gang leader waved his rifle again. "Tie them up and let's get out of here."

Henry fetched rope from his saddlebag and tied

Spence's hands behind him, then turned to Maggie. He eyed her warily, as if afraid to come too closer.

"Sorry, ma'am. I got to tie you up. But first, you gotta give me your money."

Maggie felt Spence's gaze boring into her. She ignored him. "My handbag is inside the stagecoach."

Henry slipped behind her and tied her wrists. Maggie pressed her lips together to keep from crying out as the rough material dug into her flesh.

She watched helplessly as the boy hopped into the stagecoach and emerged with her handbag.

"Excuse me?" she called. "But, if you don't mind, could you leave me just a little money?"

"For chrissake ..." Spence mumbled.

Henry looked down at the handbag. "I don't think I'm allowed to do that, ma'am."

"Well, then, at least leave me the bag itself."

"I don't know ..."

"Do you feel you must take it? Why?" Maggie asked. "Is it some sort of trophy? A keepsake? Do you feel compelled to take everything you possibly can, as a way, perhaps, to make up for no longer having your mother?"

Henry frowned, then shook his head and threw Spence a sympathetic look. "Good luck."

"Wait!" Maggie called, as he walked away. "If you could just tell me—"

"Shut the hell up!" Spence roared.

Maggie pressed her lips together and narrowed her eyes at him, then jerked his chin and turned away.

The outlaws mounted up. Maggie's stomach lurched. They rode off with the four-horse team from the stagecoach, as well as nearly every cent she had in the world.

Not only that, but they'd left her trussed like a Christmas goose, alone in the wilderness, miles from civilization, in the company of this dreadful Mr. Spence Harding.

Perhaps if she'd thought faster she could have talked them out of leaving her here like this. If only she'd had more time to speak with them, question them, she surely could have understood them better. And with understanding came communication and, eventually, agreement—or so her father always said.

Maggie's heart sank. Still, that wasn't her biggest blunder today. She should have paid better attention to the outlaws. Studied their technique. After all, she wasn't that much different from them.

Not considering that she'd traveled all the way from New York, bound for the town of Marlow, Colorado, for the sole purpose of pulling off the most daring deed humanity had ever witnessed.

Historical Romance Novels

By Dorothy Howell, also writing as Judith Stacy

Jared's Runaway Woman
The Hired Husband
The One Month Marriage
Maggie and the Law
Cheyenne Wife
Married by Midnight
The Widow's Little Secret
The Nanny
The Last Bride in Texas
The Blushing Bride
Written in the Heart
The Dreammaker
The Heart of a Hero
The Marriage Mishap
Outlaw Love

Stay For Christmas, featuring "A Place to Belong"
Spring Brides, featuring "Three Brides and a
Wedding Dress"

A Hero's Kiss, featuring "Wild West Wager"
One Christmas Wish, featuring "Christmas Wishes"
Anna's Treasure
Tea Time
Defiant Enchantress

More information is available about Dorothy's
historical romances at www.JudithStacy.com

Made in the USA
Lexington, KY
07 April 2015